INVADERS
FROM
RIGEL

INVADERS
FROM
RIGEL

Fletcher Pratt

AIRMONT

AIRMONT PUBLISHING COMPANY, INC.
22 EAST 60TH STREET · NEW YORK 22

INVADERS FROM RIGEL

An AIRMONT BOOK published by arrangement with
Thomas Bouregy and Company, Inc.

PRINTING HISTORY

Bouregy edition published April, 1960
Airmont edition published January, 1964

©, Copyright, 1960, by Fletcher Pratt

All rights reserved.

PUBLISHED SIMULTANEOUSLY IN THE DOMINION OF CANADA
BY THE RYERSON PRESS, TORONTO

PRINTED IN THE UNITED STATES OF AMERICA
BY THE COLONIAL PRESS INC., CLINTON, MASSACHUSETTS

AIRMONT PUBLISHING CO., INC., 22 East 60th St., New York 22, N.Y.

Murray Lee woke abruptly, the memory of the sound that had roused him drumming at the back of his head, though his conscious mind had been beyond its ambit. His first sensation was an overpowering stiffness in every muscle—a feeling of having been pounded all over, though his memory supplied no clue to the reason for such a sensation. Painfully he turned over in bed and felt the left elbow where the ache seemed to center. He received the most tremendous shock of his life.

The motion was attended by a creaking clang and the elbow felt exceedingly like a complex wheel.

He sat up to make sure he was awake, tossed the offending arm free of the covers. The motion produced another clang and the arm revealed itself to his astonished gaze as a system of metal bands, bound at the elbow by the mechanism he had felt before and crowned, where the fingers should be, by steely talons terminating in rubber-like fingertips. Yet there seemed to be no lack of feeling in the member.

For a few seconds he stared, open-mouthed, then lifted the other arm. It was the right-hand counterpart of the device he had been gazing at. He essayed to move one, then the other— the shining fingers obeyed his thought as though they were flesh and blood.

A sense of expectant fear gripped Lee as he lifted one of the hands to unbutton his pajamas. He was not deceived in his half-formed expectation—where the ribs clothed in a respectable amount of muscle should have been, a row of glistening metal plates appeared.

Dreaming? Drunk? A dreadful idea that he might be insane struck him and he leaped from the bed to confront a mirror. His feet struck the floor with a portentous bang and each step produced a squeak and clank—and he faced the mirror, the familiar mirror before which he had shaved for years. With utter stupefaction he saw an iron countenance above which a stiff brush of wire hair projected ludicrously.

One does not go mad at such moments. The shock takes time to sink in. "At all events I may as well get dressed," he remarked to himself.

Dressing was a process prolonged by an examination of himself and the discovery that he was a most efficient metal machine. He rather admired the smoothness of the hip joints and the way the sliding parts of his arms fitted together, was agreeably surprised to find that in the metalizing process his toes had become prehensile. Just for the fun of it he pulled one shoe on with the opposite foot.

It was not until Murray Lee was nearly dressed that he realized that the wonted noise of New York, which reached as a throaty undertone to the forty-eighth story of the modern apartment building, was somehow absent. Surely at this hour—he glanced at the clock. It had stopped at a quarter to two. No help there. His watch was inexplicably missing. Probably Ben had borrowed it.

That was the idea. Ben Ruby, with whom he occupied the duplex apartment in the penthouse of the Arbuckle Building, was a scientist of sorts—mainly engaged in the analysis of gland extract samples for millionaires distrustful of their rejuvenators these days—he would be able to explain.

Lee stepped across to the door and dropped the brass knocker, a little timorous at the sound of his own thudding steps. The door was snatched open with unexpected suddenness by a caricature of Ben in metal—as complete a machine as Murray himself, but without most of his clothes.

"Come in! Come in!" his friend bellowed in a voice with an oddly phonographic quality to it. "You look great. Iron Man MacGinnity! What did you put on clothes for? As useful as pants on a rock-drill. I have breakfast."

"What is it? Am I crazy—are you—or are we both?" Lee asked.

"Of course not. Greatest thing that ever happened. The big comet. They said she was radioactive but most of 'em wouldn't believe it. Now look what it did." Murray Lee remembered vaguely some newspaper palaver about a giant comet that was going to strike Earth.

"Everybody's turned to metal. Nize machinery, ate oop all de axlegrease. You need oil. Stick around."

Ben Ruby disappeared into the bowels of the apartment, the sound of his footsteps ringing enormous in the vast silence. In an instant he was back with a radio battery in one hand and an oil-can in the other.

"Sorry, no grease on tap," he remarked briskly. "Typewriter oil." He went to work busily, squirting drops of oil into Lee's new metallic joints. "Connect this thing up yourself. It fills you with what it takes." He indicated the battery with an extended toe. "One arm and the opposite leg. There seems to be a resistance chamber in us somewhere that collects the juice."

Without in the least understanding what it was all about, Murray Lee followed instructions.

It was the most singular meal he had ever partaken of but he found it curiously invigorating.

"How about another? No? Have you seen anybody else? It finished most of them."

"Will you sit down and tell me consecutively what it's all about before I bash you?" asked Murray, petulantly.

"Some sort of a special extra-radioactive gas-storm connected with the comet, I think, though I can't be sure. It's made machines of all of us, now and forever more. We'll live on electric current after this and won't have to bother about little things like doctors—if we can find a good mechanic. But it killed a lot of people. Come along, I'll show you."

His hand rang on Murray's arm as he grasped it to lead the way. The hall was portentously dark and Ben pulled him straight across it to the door marked *Fire Exit.*

"Elevator?" queried Murray.

"No go. No power."

"Oh, Lord, forty-eight stories to walk."

"You'll get used to it." They were clanking to the landing of the floor below and Ben, without the slightest compunction, pushed boldly into the door of the apartment there. The lock showed signs of being forced.

"Oh, I broke it in," Ben answered Murray's unspoken query. "Thought I might be able to help, but it was no use. That fat woman lives here—you know, the one that used to sniff at us in the elevator when we went on a bender."

Any qualms Murray felt about looking on the naked face of death were perfunctorily laid to rest as the scientist led him into the room occupied by the late lady of the elevator. She lay solidly in her bed, the weight of her body sagging the bed grotesquely toward its center. Instead of the clean-running mechanical devices which marked the appearance of the two friends, she was nothing but lumps and bumps, a bulging ugly cast-iron statue, distending the cheap "silk" nightdress.

"See?" said Ben, calmly. "The transmutation wasn't complete. Prob'ly didn't get it as strong as we did. Look, the window's closed. Come along."

Murray lingered. "Isn't there anything we can do?"

"Not a thing," said Ben, cheerfully. "All she's good for is to stand in the park and look at. Come along. We've got a lot of stairs to go down. We're too noisy—need a good bath in non-rusting oil."

They reached the street level after an aeon of stairs, Ben leading the way to the corner drug store. All about them was a complete silence. Fleecy white clouds sailed across the little ribbon of blue visible at the top of the canyon of the New York city street.

"Lucky it's a nice day," said Ben, boldly stepping into the drug store, the door of which stood open. "We'll have to figure out this rainy weather thing. It's going to be a problem."

Within, the drug store presented the same phenomena of arrested development as the apartment of the fat lady at the forty-seventh story. A cast-iron statue of a soda-clerk leaned on the fountain in an attitude of studied negligence, its lips parted as though addressing some words to the equally metalic figure of a girl which faced him across the counter. On her steely

features was a film of powder and the caked and curling remains of her lipstick showed she had been there for some time.

"By the way," Murray asked, "have you any idea what day
it is, and how long we were—under the influence? It couldn't
have happened overnight."

"Why not?" came Ben's voice from the rear of the store.
"Say, old dear, rummage around some of those drawers for rubber gloves, will you? I'd hate to run into high voltage with this
outfit."

"Here they are," said Lee. "Let's go. What's the next step?"
They were outside.

"Rubber shoes, I fancy," said Ben as his feet skidded on
the pavement. "Let's take a taxi there and go find a shoe store."

Together they managed to slide the cast-iron taxi driver from
his seat (Murray was surprised at how easily he was able to lift
a weight he could not have budged in his flesh-and-blood days),
deposited him on the curb and climbed in. The key was fortunately in the switch.

As they swung around the corner into Madison Avenue Lee
gave an exclamation. A scene of ruin and desolation met their
ey.. . or three ....d telescoped and an auto or so had
piled into the wreckage. All about ... . iron forms of the
passengers in these conveyances, frozen in the var... ...titudes
they had assumed at the moment of the change, and from one
or two of them thin streamers of metal showed where blood had
flowed forth before it had been irretrievably crystallized to
metal.

Murray Lee suddenly realized that an enormous amount of
machinery had gone to smash everywhere when the guiding
hands had been removed and the guiding brains frozen to useless metal. He gave a little shudder.

They swung round before a shoe store with grating brakes.
The door was locked but Ben, lifting his foot, calmly kicked a
hole in the show window.

"No use asking permission. If the proprietor of this place is
still alive anywhere it will be easy enough to settle up for the
damage. If he isn't we have as good a right to it as anybody."

The new toes, which appeared to be longer than those he remembered, made fitting a difficulty and Murray split two or
three shoes before he got a pair on.

"What next?" he asked. "I feel like a drink."

"No use," said Ben. "You're on the wagon for good. Alcohol
would play merry hell with your metal-work. The best thing is
to find out how many people we are. For all we know we're the
only ones in the world. This thing seems to have knocked out
everybody along the street level. Let's try some of the taller
apartment buildings and see if we can find more penthouse dwel-
lers."

"Or maybe the others came to before us and went away."

"True," Ben said. "Anyhow, look-see." He led the way to the taxi.

"Wait," said Murray. "What's that?"

Over the sound of the starting engine came the echo of heavy footsteps, muffled by shoes.

"Hey! This way!" shouted Ben The footsteps tentatively approached the corner. Murray ran forward, then stopped in amazement. The newcomer was a girl—or would have been a girl had she not been all metal and machinery like themselves. To his eyes, still working on flesh-and-blood standards, she was anything but good-looking. She was fully and formally dressed, save that she wore no hat—the high pile of tangled wire that crowned her head made this obviously impossible.

"Oh, what *has* happened?" she cried at them. "What can I do? I took a drink of water and it hurt."

"Everything's all right. Just a little metal transformation," said Ben. "Stick around, I'll get you some oil. You squeak." He was off down the street in a clatter, leaving Murray with the girl.

"Permit me to introduce myself," he said. "I am—or was—Murray Lee. My friend, who has gone to get you some oil, is Benjamin Franklin Ruby. He thinks the big comet which hit the earth contained radioactive gas that made us all into metal. Did you live in a penthouse?"

She eyed him darkly. "Somebody told you," she said. "I'm Gloria Rutherford and we have the top floor of the Sherry-Netherland but all the rest were away when this happened. Pardon me, it hurts me to talk."

There came a crash from down the street, indicating that Ben was forcing another store, and in a minute he was back with a handful of bottles. With a flourish he offered one to the girl.

"Only castor, but it's the best the market affords," he said. "What we need is a good garage but there aren't many around here. Go ahead, drink her down, it's all right," he assured the girl.

Following his own recommendation he tipped up one of the bottles and drank a deep draught, then calmly proceeded to douse himself head to foot with the remainder.

Gloria made a little grimace, then tried it. "Thank you," she said, setting the bottle down. "I didn't think it was possible anybody could like the stuff except in a magazine ad. Now tell me, where are all the other people and what do we do?"

"Do?" asked Ben. "Find 'em. Anybody else in your neck of the woods?"

She shook her head. Murray noticed that the joints of her neck rattled. "Paulson—that's my maid—was the only other person in our apartment and she seems to be even more solid-iron in the head than usual—like this lot." She swung her hand

round in an expressive gesture toward the image of a policeman, which was directing two similar images to pause at the
curb.

"How about a bonfire?" suggested Murray. "That's the way
the Indians or South Africans or somebody attract attention."

"What could we burn?" asked Ben. "A building, of course.
Why not? Property doesn't mean anything any more with all
the property owners dead."

"I know," said Gloria, falling into the spirit of his suggestion.
"The old Metropolitan Opera House. That eyesore has worried
me for the last five years."

The suggestion was endorsed with enthusiasm. They climbed
into the taxi and twenty minutes later were hilariously kindling
a blaze in the back-stage section of the old building, running out
of it with childish delight to watch the pillar of smoke grow and
spread.

Murray sighed as they sat on the curb across the street. "This
is the only time I've ever been as close as I wanted to be to a big
fire."

"What if it sets fire to the whole city?" asked Gloria.

Ben shrugged. "What if?" he replied. "Doesn't mean anything. Bet there aren't more than a couple of dozen people
alive. But I don't think it will. Modern construction in most of
these places is too fireproof."

"Look, there's a bird," said Gloria, indicating a solid metal
pigeon, fixed like the human inhabitants of the city in his last
position in life at the edge of the curb. "By the way, what do
᠁t? Do we live on Castor oil all the time?"

Two

The conversation turned into ᠁ ᠁cussion of the possibilities
of their new form. Whether they wo᠁᠁ ᠁eed sleep was a moot
point and they were discussing the adv᠁᠁ ᠁᠁ity of training
mechanics as doctors when the first footsteps announced themselves.

They belonged to a man whose face, ornamented by a neat
Van Dyke in wire, gave him the appearance of a physician of
the more fleshy life, but who turned out to be a lawyer named
Roberts. He was delighted with the extraordinary youthfulness
and vitality he felt in the new incarnation.

Fully dressed in morning clothes he bore the information
that he was one of a group of four who had achieved the metal
transformation atop the French building. He promptly plunged
into a discussion of technicalities with Ben that left the other
two out of it and they moved off to the Seventh Avenue side of
the building to see whether any more people were visible.

"Do you miss the people much?" asked Murray.

"Not a bit," Gloria said. "My chief emotion is delight over not having to go to the de la Poers' tea tomorrow afternoon. Though I suppose we will miss them as time goes on."

"Well," Murray sighed, "that tripe is all through with now. What do you say we get back and see how the rest are getting along?"

They found them still in the midst of their argument.

". . . evidently some substance so volatile that the mere contact with animal tissue causes a reaction that leaves nothing of either the element or the tissue," Ben was saying. "You note that these metal bands reproduce the muscles almost perfectly."

"Yes," the lawyer replied, "but they are too flexible to be any metal I know of. I'm willing to grant your wider knowledge of chemistry but it doesn't seem reasonable. All I can think of is that some outside agency has interfered. These joints, for instance"—he touched Ben's elbow—"and what about the little rubber pads on your fingers and toes and the end of your nose?"

There was a universal motion on the part of the others to feel of their noses. It was as the lawyer had said—they were, like the fingers and toes, certainly very much like rubber—and movable!

"Don't know," said Ben. "Who did it, though? That's what boggles your scheme. Everybody's changed to metal and nobody left to make the changes you mention. However, let's go get the rest of your folks. I wonder if we ought to have weapons. You two wait here."

He clanked off the lawyer to the taxi. A moment later the tooting of the horn announced their return. The party consisted, besides Roberts himself, of his daughter Ola Mae, a girl of sixteen, petulant over the fact that her high-heeled shoes were already breaking down under her weight—a Japanese servant named Yoshio—and Mrs. Roberts, one of those tall and billowy women of the earlier life who, to the irritation of the men, turned out to be the strongest of any of them. Fat, apparently, had no metallic equivalent, and her ample proportions now consisted of bands of metal that made her extraordinarily powerful.

With these additions the little group adjourned to Times Square to watch the clouds of smoke rising above the ruins of the opera house.

"What next?" asked Gloria, seating herself on the curbstone.

"Look for more people," said Murray. "Surely we can't be the only frogs in the puddle."

"Why not?" asked Ben, with a swing of his arm toward the wreckage-strewn square. "You forget that this catastrophe has probably wiped out all the animal life of the world and we seven owe our survival to some fortunate chance."

The Japanese touched him on the arm. "Perhaps sir can inform inquirer, in such case, what is curious avian object?" He pointed upward.

They heard the beat of wings as he spoke and looked up together to see, soaring fifty feet past their heads a strange parody of a bird with four distinct wings, a long feathered tail and bright intelligent eyes set in a dome-like head.

There was a moment of excited babbling.

"What is it?"

"Never saw anything like it before."

"Did the comet do *that* to chickens?" And then, as the strange creature disappeared among the forest of spires to the east, the voice of the lawyer, used to such tumults, asserted its mastery over the rest.

"I think," he said, "that whatever that bird is the first thing to be done is find a headquarters of some kind and establish a mode of life."

"How about finding more people?" asked Gloria. "The more the merrier—and there may be some who don't know how nice castor oil is." She smiled a metallic smile.

"The fire . . ." began Ben.

"It would keep some people away."

They debated the point for several minutes, finally deciding that since those present had all come from the top floors or penthouses of tall buildings the search should be confined to such localities. Each was to take a car—there were any number for the taking around Times Square—and cover a certain section of the city, rallying at sundown at the Times building, where Ola Mae and Murray, who could not drive, were to be left.

Roberts was the first one back. He had found no one but had a curious tale. In the upper floors of the Waldorf three of the big windows were smashed and in one corner of the room, amid a maze of chairs fantastically torn as though by a playful giant, was a pile of soft cloths.

In the midst of this pile, four big eggs reposed. He had picked up one of the eggs and, after weighing the advisability of bringing it with him, decided he had more important things to do. The owners of the nest did not appear.

As he emerged from the building, however, the quick motion of a shadow across the street caused him to look up in time to catch a glimpse of one of the four-winged birds they had seen before; and just as he was driving the car away his ears were assailed by a torrent of screeches and "skrawks" from the homecomer. He did not look up until the shadow fell across him again when he perceived the bird was following close behind him, flying low and apparently debating the advisability of attacking him.

Roberts waved his arms and shouted. It had not the slightest effect on the bird, which, now that it was closer, he perceived to be moving its hind wings alone, holding its fore-wings out like those of an airplane. He had wished for a weapon of some kind. Lacking one, he drew the car up to the curb and ran into a building.

The bird alighted outside and began to peck the door in but by the time it got through Roberts had climbed a maze of stairs. Though he could hear it screaming throatily behind him it did not find him and eventually gave up the search.

The end of this remarkable tale was delivered to an enlarged audience.

Gloria had arrived, bringing a chubby little man who announced himself as F. W. Stevens.

"The boy plunger?"

"Well, I operate in Wall Street," Stevens replied rather stiffly.

Ben came with three recruits. At the sight of the first Murray gasped. Even in the metal caricature, he had no difficulty in recognizing the high bald forehead, the thin jaws and toothbrush moustache of Walter Beeville, greatest living naturalist.

Before dark the others were back—Yoshio with one new acquisition and Mrs. Roberts, whose energy paralleled her strength, with no less than four, among them an elaborately gowned woman who proved to be Marta Lami, the Hungarian dancer who had been the sensation of New York at the time of the catastrophe.

They gathered in the Times Square drug store in a strange babble of phonographic voices and clang of metal parts against the stone floor and soda fountains. It was Roberts who secured a position behind one of these dispensers of liquid soothing-syrup and rapped for order.

"I think the first thing to be done," he said when the voices had grown quiet in answer to his appeal, "is to organize the group of people here and search for more. If it had not been for the kindness of Mr. Ruby here, my family and I would not have known about the necessity of using oil on this new mechanical makeup nor of the value of electrical current as food. There may be others in the city in the same state. What is the —ah—sense of the gathering on this topic?"

Stevens was the first to speak. "It's more important to organize and elect a president," he said.

"A very good idea," commented Roberts.

"Well then," said Stevens ponderously, "I move we proceed to elect officers and form a corporation."

"Second the motion," said Murray.

"Pardon me." It was the voice of Beeville the naturalist. "I don't think we ought to adopt any formal organization yet. It hardly seems necessary. We are practically in the golden age,

with all the resources of an immense city at the disposal of—
fourteen people. And we know very little about ourselves. All
the medical and biological science of the world must be discarded and built up again.

"At this very moment we may be suffering from the lack of
something that is absolutely necessary to our existence—though
I admit I cannot imagine what it could be. I think the first thing
to do is to investigate our possibilities and establish the science
of mechanical medicine. As to the rest of our details of existence, they don't matter much at present."

A murmur of approval went round the room and Stevens
looked somewhat put out. "We could hardly adopt anarchy as
a form of government."

"Oh, yes, we could," said Marta Lami. "Hurray for anarchy.
The Red Flag forever. Free love, free beer, no work!"

"Yes," said Gloria, "what's the use of all this metalizing,
anyway?"

"Say," came a deep and raucous voice from one of the new-
comers. "Why don't we have just a straw boss for a while till
we see how things work out? If anyone gets fresh the straw boss
can jump him or kick him out but those that stick with the
crowd have to listen to him. How's that?"

There was a clanging round of metallic applause as three or
four people clapped their hands.

"There is a motion . . ." began Roberts.

"Oh, tie a can to it," said Gloria "I nominate Ben Ruby as
head man of the colony of New York for—three months. Everybody that's for it, stick up your hands."

Eleven hands went up. Gloria looked around and concentrated
her gaze on Stevens. "Won't you join us, Mr. Stevens?"

"I don't think this is the way to do things. It's altogether irregular and no permanent good can result from it. However, I
will act with the rest."

"And you, Yoshio?"

"I am uncertain that permission is granted to this miserable worm to vote."

"Certainly. We're all starting from scratch. Who else is
there? What about you, Mr. Lee?"

"I know him too well."

The rest of the opposition dissolved in laughter and Ben
made his way to the place at the counter vacated by Roberts.

"The first thing we need is have some light," Ruby said. "Does
anyone know where candles can be had around here? I suppose
there ought to be some in the drug store across the street but I
don't know where and there's no light to look by."

"How about flashlights? There's an electrical and video store
up the block."

"Fine. Murray, you go look. Now, Miss Roberts, will you be
our secretary? I think the first thing to do is to get down the

name and occupation of everyone here. That will give us a start toward finding out what we can do. Ready? Now you, Miss Rutherford, first."

"My name is Gloria Rutherford and I can't do anything but play tennis, drink and drive a car."

The rest of the replies followed. F. W. Stevens, Wall Street —Theodore Roberts, lawyer—Archibald Tholfsen, chess-player —H. M. Dangerfield, editor—Francis X. O'Hara, trucking business. "Are you a mechanic, too?" asked Ben.

"Well, not a first class one but I know a little about machinery."

"Good, you're appointed our doctor."

Paul Farrelly, publisher—Albert F. Massey, artist—the voices droned on in the uncertain illumination of the flashlights.

"Very well then," said Ben at the conclusion of the list. "The first thing I'll do is appoint Walter Beeville director of research. Fact number one for him is that we aren't going to need much of any sleep. I don't feel the need of it at all and I don't seem to see any signs among you.

"O'Hara will help him on the mechanical side—I suggest that as Mr. Beeville will need to observe all of us we make the Rockefeller Institute our headquarters. He will have the apparatus there to carry on his work. Let's go."

Three.

They whirled away to the east side of the city and up Second Avenue like a triumphal cortege, blissfully disregarding the dead traffic lights, though now and then they had to dodge the ruins of some truck or taxi. At Forty-ninth Street Ben's car, in the lead, swung in to the curb and pulled up.

"What is it?" . . . "Is this the place?" . . . "Anything wrong?"

An illuminating voice floated up. "Electric store—get all the flashlights and batteries you can. We're going to need them."

A few moments later they were at the great institution, strangely dark and silent now after all its years of ministering to the sick, with a line of rust showing redly on the tall iron fence that surrounded the grounds. They trooped into the reception room, flickering their lights here and there like fireflies. Ben mounted a chair.

"Just a minute, folks," he began. "I want to say something. What we have to do here is build civilization up all over again. Undoubtedly there are more people alive—if not in New York then in other places. We have two jobs—to get in touch with them and to find out what we can do. Mr. Beeville is going to find out about the second one for us but we can do a lot without waiting for him.

"In the first place there's that funny-looking bird we all saw and that chased Roberts. There may be others like it and a lot of new queer forms of animal life around that would be dangerous to us. Therefore, I think it's in line to get some weapons. Miss Lami, you and Mr. Tholfsen are delegated to dig up a hardware store and find guns and cartridges. Now for the rest, I'm open to suggestions."

Everybody spoke at once. "Wait a minute," said Ben. "Let's take things in order. What was your idea, Mr. Stevens?"

"Organize regular search parties."

"A good idea, too. We don't even need to wait for daylight. Everybody who can drive, get a car and trot along."

"X-ray machines are going to be awfully useful in my work," offered Beeville. "I wonder if there isn't some way of getting enough current to run one."

"As far as I remember this building supplies its own current. Murray, you and Massey trot down and get a fire up under one of the boilers. Anything else?"

"Yes," came from Dangerfield, the editor. "It seems to me that the first thing anyone else in the world would try to do if he found himself made into a tin doll like this is to get hold of a radio. How about opening up a broadcasting station?"

"I don't know whether you can get enough power but you can try. Go to it. Do you know anything about radio?"

"A little."

"All right. Pick whoever you want for an assistant and try it out. Any more ideas?"

"What day is it?" asked Ola Mae Roberts.

Nobody had thought of it and it suddenly dawned on the assemblage that the last thing they remembered was when the snow on the roof-tops bespoke a chilly February while now all the trees were in leaf and the air was redolent of spring.

"Why—I don't know," said Ben. "Anybody here got any ideas on how to find out?"

"It would take an experienced astronomer and some calculation to determine with accuracy," said Beeville. "We'd better set an arbitrary date."

"Okay. Then it's May 1, 1964. That's ahead of time but it will take that long to find out what it really is."

The assumption that sleep would be unnecessary proved correct. All night long cars roared up to the door and away again on their quests. The number of people found was small—the cream had apparently been gathered that morning.

O'Hara brought in a metallic scrubwoman from one of the downtown buildings, the tines that represented her teeth showing stains of rust where she had incautiously drunk water.

Stevens turned up with a slow-voiced young man who proved to be Georgios Pappagourdas, attache of the Greek consulate, whose name had been in the papers in connection with a sensational divorce case. Mrs. Roberts came in with two men, one of them J. Sterling Vanderschoof, president of the steamship lines which bore his name.

At dawn, Dangerfield came in. He had set up a powerful receiving set by means of storage batteries but could find no messages on the air and could find no source of power sufficient for him to broadcast.

The morning, therefore, saw another and somewhat less optimistic conference. As it was breaking up Ben said, "You Tholfsen, take Stevens, Vanderschoof and Lee and get a truck, will you? You'll find one about half a block down the street. Go up to one of the coal pits and get some fuel for our boilers. We haven't too large a supply."

There was a clanking of feet as they left and Ben turned into the laboratory where Beeville was working with the scrubwoman as a subject.

"Something interesting here," said the naturalist, looking up as he entered. "The outer surface of this metal appears to be rustproof but when you get water on the inside things seem to go. It acts like a specially annealed compound of some kind. And look . . ."

He seized one of the arms of his subject, and yanked at the outer layer of metal bands that composed it. The band stretched like one of rubber and she gave a slight squeal as it snapped back.

"I don't know of any metal that has that flexibility. Do you? Why . . ."

The door swung open and they turned to see Murray and Tholfsen.

"Beg pardon for interrupting the sacred panjandrum," said the former, "but Stevens and Vanderschoof don't want to play with us."

"Oh, cripes," remarked Ben carefully and started for the door, the other two following him.

He found the recalcitrants soon enough. The Wall Street man was seated across a doctor's desk from Vanderschoof and looked up calmly from an interrupted conversation as Ben entered.

"Thought I asked you two to go with the boys for some coal," said Ben. "My mistake. I meant to."

"You did. I'm not going."

Ben's eyes narrowed. "Why not?"

"This is the United States of America, young man. I don't recognize that I am under your orders or anyone else's. If you think you are going to get us to accept any dictatorship you've got another guess coming. As I was saying . . ." He turned back to Vanderschoof. Murray took a step toward him.

"Leave me alone, boys, I can handle this," said Ben, waving the other two back. "Mr. Stevens"—the broker looked up with insolent politeness—"this is not the United States but the colony of New York. Conditions have changed and the sooner you recognize that the better for all of us. We are trying to rebuild civilization from the ruins. If you don't share in the work you shall not share in the benefits."

"And what are you going to do about it?"

"Put you out."

There was a quick flash and Ben was staring into the business end of a Luger automatic, gripped tightly in the broker's hand. "Oh no you won't. You forget that you made this anarchy yourself when you refused to have a president. Now get out of here quick and let me talk with my friend."

For a moment the air was heavy with tension. Then Vanderschoof smiled—a superior smile. Stevens' eyes blinked and in that blink Ben charged. As he moved Murray and Tholfsen followed.

There was a report like a clap of thunder in the narrow room, a tremendous ringing clang as the bullet struck the metal plate of Ben's shoulder and caromed to the ceiling, whirling him around against the desk and to the floor with the force of its impact. Murray leaped across his prostrate body, striking at the gun and knocking it down just in time to send the second shot wild. Tholfsen stumbled and fell across Ben.

Ben was up first, diving for Murray and Stevens, now locked in close grapple, but the chess-player's action was more effective. From his prone position he reached up, grabbed Stevens' legs and pulled them from under him, bringing him down with a crash just as Ben's added weight made the struggle hopelessly one-sided.

In a moment more, the dictator of the New York colony was sitting on his subject's chest while Murray held his arms. Vanderschoof sat cowering in his chair.

"Get some wire," gasped Ben. "Don't think cloth will hold him."

Tholfsen released his hold on the legs and climbed to his feet. "Watch the other one, Murray," said Ben.

"Now, you listen." He addressed the man beneath him. "We could tie you up and lay you away to pickle until you died for the lack of whatever you need or we could turn you over to Beeville to cut up as a specimen. And by heaven"—glaring with a kind of suppressed fury—"I wouldn't hesitate to do it! You're jeopardizing the safety of the whole community."

The grim face beneath him showed neither a fear nor contrition. "If I let you go and give you a car and a couple of batteries, will you promise to clear out and never come back?"

Stevens laughed shortly. "Do you think you can bluff me? No."

"All right, Tholfsen, get his feet first," said Ben as the chess-player reappeared with a length of light-cord he had wrenched from somewhere. The feet kicked energetically but the task was accomplished and the arms secured likewise. "You watch him," said Ben, "while I get a car around."

"What are you going to do?" asked Vanderschoof.

"Throw him in the river!" declared Ben. "Let him get out of that."

"But you can't do that," protested the steamship man. "It's inhuman."

"Bring him outside, boys," said Ben without deigning to reply as he clanged out to the car.

They lifted the helpless man into the back seat and with a man on either side of him started for Queensboro Bridge.

Halfway down the span Ben brought the taxi round with a flourish and climbed out, the other two lifting Stevens between them; they set down their burden at the rail.

"Over with him!" said Ben remorsely. They bent . . .

"I give up," said Stevens in a strangely husky voice. Murray and Tholfsen paused.

"Did you hear what I said?" said Ben. "Over with him!"

They heaved. "Stop!" screamed the broker. "I'll give up. I'll go. Oh-h-h!" The last was a scream as Ben laid a detaining hand on Murray's arm.

"Let him down, boys," he said quietly. "Now listen, Stevens. I don't want to be hard on you—but we've got to have unanimity. You're done. Take a car and clear out. If I let you go now will you promise to stay away?"

"Yes," said the Wall Street man. "Anything, only for heaven's sake don't do that!"

"All right," said Ben.

As they were loading the banker in the car for the return trip a thought struck Murray. "By the way, Ben," he remarked, "didn't he nick you with that gun?"

"That's right," said Ben, "he did." He gazed down at the long bright scratch in the heavy metal that covered his shoulder joint. It was uninjured.

Four

But when Tholfsen and Murray returned with the coal, Vanderschoof was missing as well as Stevens. That evening, when the car in which Marta Lami had accompanied Roberts on the exploration of the Brooklyn Heights district drew up at the Institute, it had only one occupant.

"What happened to Miss Lami?" asked Ben.

Roberts gazed at him, surprised. "Did you send them? While we were at the St. George Hotel a car came along with Stevens and two of those men in it. One was the Greek. They spoke to

her for a minute and she said they brought a message from
you that she was to go with them."

"M-hm," said Ben. "I see. Well, as long as they don't come
back, it's all right."

The car whirled along the Albany Post Road in a silence that
was indicative of the rivalry that had already sprung up between Stevens and Vanderschoof. As for Pappagourdas he found
himself demoted to the position of a yes man.

They had provided themselves with a liberal supply of guns
and ammunition and had raided store after store until they had
acquired a considerable supply of currency.

"This is the Bear Mountain Bridge, isn't it?" said the dancer.
"Let's stop at West Point and pick up a cadet. They're so or-
namental."

Stevens glanced at her sourly from the wheel. "We've got to
hurry if we want to get to Albany," he said.

"Still," offered Vanderschoof protectingly, "why not stop
at the Point? We might find some people there. I know Colonel
Grayson. Played golf with him last summer. When I holed
out an eighteen-footer at the seventh, he was so mad he wouldn't
speak to me all the rest of the afternoon. It was the turning
point of the battle. Ha, ha!"

Stevens, with a grunt, swung the wheel round and began the
ascent of the long bridge ramp. "Isn't that a bird?"

"The high muckamuck said something about birds last night,"
said the dancer, "but he's such a Holy Joe that I didn't pay any
attention."

"Aren't the birds all dead?" asked the Greek, respectfully. "I
saw some in the . . . . my window and they were turned
to iron."

The car coughed to the rise, ... slid across the
bridge.

"It *is* a bird," said the dancer, "and what a . . .
at the ostrich."

Pappagourdas and Vanderschoof followed her pointing finger.
They saw, a couple of hundred feet behind and above them,
the widespread wings and heavy body of the same type of four-
winged bird Roberts had encountered. Vanderschoof tugged at
his pocket. "Maybe it'll come close enough to give us a shot."

The bird was certainly gaining on them. As it drew nearer
they could make out the high-domed unbird-like head with
pop-eyes fixed in a permanent expression of astonishment, the
short bill, slightly hooked at the tip, the huge expanse of the
wings. It seemed to be inspecting them as a smaller avian might
inspect a bug.

As it drew nearer it swooped to within a couple of dozen feet
of the car. They noticed that its feet, folded back beneath the
body, had a metallic luster. Then Vanderschoof fired with a

could see where the big rock had struck the right bumper, tearing a foot or two of it loose to trail on the road.

"Wait," he cried but Stevens shook his head.

They had a bit of luck at this point. The hunt for more stones or something of the kind delayed their enemies and when they next saw the birds winging up behind them the white classical lines of the West Point administration building already loomed ahead, clear in the gathering gloom.

Stevens turned in, swung the car around at the door, halted it with screaming brakes, just as the first of the birds overhead overshot the mark and turned to come back. In an instant the banker was out of the car, dragging at Marta Lami's hand.

Vanderschoof climbed nimbly out the other side and ran around the car toward the door of the building but the Greek missed his footing and fell prone just as one of the birds dived down with a yell of triumph and dropped his stone accurately onto the struggling man.

"*Run!*" shouted Stevens.

"But the Greek," panted Vanderschoof as they climbed the steps.

"Heck with him. Or here—wait." Stevens turned and thrust his fist through the glass upper portion of the door. Out in the dusk the three bird-forms were settling round their fallen foe.

The flash of the banker's gun stabbed the night and was answered by a scream. Before he could take aim again, with a quick beat of wings they were gone. When he ran out a few moments later, he found that Pappagourdas was gone also.

He found the others on one of the benches in the outer office of the building, the girl with her face buried in her hands in an agony of fright and reaction. Vanderschoof, too old and cool a hand to give way in this fashion, looked up.

"What are they, Stevens?"

The Wall Street man shrugged his shoulders helplessly. "I don't know," he said. "some new kind of highpower bird that developed while we were all being made into machines by that comet, I suppose. It's terrible. They've got the Greek."

"Can't we get after them? There ought to be airplanes here."

"In this light? Can you fly one? I can't and I don't imagine the little girl here can."

The "little girl" lifted her head. "What did we come to this joint for anyhow?" she asked. "To hang crepe on the chandeliers?"

The words had the effect of an electric shock.

"Why, of course," said Stevens, "we did come here to see if we could find someone, didn't we?" and turning round he pushed open the door into the next room. Nothing.

"Wait," he said. "Not much use trying to do anything tonight. We haven't any flashlights."

"What do you want us to do? Sit here and count our fingers? Go on, find a garage. You can get a light from one of the cars."

"Won't those birds see it?"

"You got a yellow streak a mile wide. Birds sleep at night."

Stevens took a half-unwilling step toward the door. "Let me come with you," said Vanderschoof, rising.

"What's the matter, papa? You got a little yellow in you, too?"

He was dignified. "Not at all. Here I'll leave my gun with you, Miss Lami."

"We'll be seeing you," said Stevens over his shoulder. "Don't worry." And they were gone.

To the dancer their absence was endless. She would have given anything for the velvet kick of a good drink—"but I suppose it would burn out my bearings," she mused.

More clearly than the rest she realized that very little was left of the old relation between the sexes. What would happen when the forceful Stevens made the discovery also?

What was that?

She listened intently. A subdued rattling, slightly metallic in character. It might be a rat—no, too mechanical. The men—probably it was them or one of them, returning. She glanced out of the window. Not there. The sound again—not from outdoors but behind her—within the room? She gripped the gun Vanderschoof had given her. Rattle, rattle. She wished furiously for a light.

The birds? No—birds sleep at night. Rattle, rattle. Persistently. She stood up, trying to pierce the gathering dimness. No, the birds would make more noise.

This sound was small, like the chatter of a mechanical rat. On slenderest tiptoes she backed cautiously across the rug toward the outer door.

Holding the gun before her firmly she stepped back, back, feeling with one hand for the door. Her hand met its smooth surface, then clicked as the metallic joints came in contact with the doorknob. She paused, breathless. Rattle, rattle, went the small sound, discouraged.

With a sudden jerk she flung the door open and tumbled down the steps, half-falling. As she fell, as though in answer to the metallic clang of her body on the stone, a long pencil of violet light sprang silently out from somewhere back in the hills, moved thrice across the sky, then faded as swiftly as it had come.

She felt the beam of a flashlight in her eyes and got up, hearing her voice with a sort of inward surprise as it babbled something slightly incoherent about, "things—in there."

Stevens' voice, rough with irritation. "What is it you're saying?" He shook her arm. "Come on, little woman, pull yourself together."

"There must be someone else around here," remarked Vanderschoof irrelevantly. "Did you see that searchlight?"

Marta Lami pulled herself up short, shaking loose the hand with a touch of the arrogance that had made her the queen of the night life of New York.

"Something in there gives me the fantods," she said. "Sounds like some guy shooting craps with himself."

Stevens laughed, somewhat forcedly. "Well, it's nothing to be scared of unless it's one of those bloody birds and if it was that he'd be taking us apart now. Come on!"

He flung the door open and plunged in, the flashlight flickering before him. Empty.

There was a door at the further end, next to the one they had investigated before. Toward this he strode, clump, clump on the carpet, and flung it open likewise. Empty again. No, there *was* something. The questing beam came to rest on a brown army tunic behind the desk, followed it up quickly to the face and there held. Staring at them with mechanical fixity was another of those simulations of the human face in metal with which they were by now so familiar. But this one was different.

For it held the balance between the walking cartoons of men in metal, such as they themselves were, and the ugly and solid statues they had seen strewn about the streets of New York.

It had the metal bands across the forehead that they possessed, above which issued the same wiry hair, in this case curiously interwoven as though subjected to great heat and melted into a single mass. The nose was all of solid metal and the eyes —the eyes—were the eyes of a statue, giving back no lustrous reflection of glass.

They paused, breathless, then stepped forward and as the beam of light shifted when Stevens moved, rattle, rattle came the sound Marta Lami had heard. And when the light went back the unseeing eyes had moved.

For a few seconds no one spoke. Then, "Good Lord, it's alive!" said Vanderschoof in a hushed voice.

Stevens broke the spell, stepping swiftly to the desk. "Can we do anything for you?" he asked. No movement came from the metal figure—only that ghastly rustle of the eyes as they turned here and there in the fixed head.

The Wall Street man lifted one of the hands, tried to flex the arm that held it. It dropped back to the desk with a crash. Yet the metal of which it was composed seemed in itself to be as pliant as that of their own arms.

"What happened to him?" asked Marta Lami in a whisper as though she feared awakening a sleeper.

Stevens shrugged. "What's happened to all of us? He's alive, I tell you. Let's get out of here. I don't like it."

"But where to?"

"Follow the Albany road," said Stevens. "We ought to move on. If those birds come back in the morning . . ."

"But what about this poor chap?" asked Marta Lami.

"Leave him. There's too much mystery about this whole business around here. You can stay here till you rot if you like. I'm clearing out."

Five

Naturally exploration of the familiar, yet unfamiliar world into which they had suddenly been thrown was the first preoccupation of the New York colonists. None of the group cared to wander far from the Institute during the first weeks, however, in view of the possible difficulty of obtaining electrical food for a long trip; and Beeville's researches on the potentialities of their new bodily form advanced so slowly that they hardly dared leave.

His discoveries in the first weeks were in fact purely negative. Farrelly, the publisher, smashed a finger in some machinery but when O'Hara turned an exact duplicate out on his lathe and Beeville attached it the new member lacked sensation and could be moved only with conscious effort—an indication that some as yet unfamiliar reaction underlay the secret of motion in their metal form.

But the greatest difficulty in the way of any activity lay in the almost abysmal ignorance of mechanical and technical arts on the part of the whole group. O'Hara was a fair mechanic, Dangerfield dabbled in radio and Farrelly could run a printing press—he published a comical parody of a newspaper on one for several days, then abandoned the effort. But beyond that their utmost accomplishment was driving a car and most of them realized how helpless the old civilization had been without its hewers of wood and drawers of water.

To remedy this condition as much as to keep them busy Ben assigned to each some branch of mechanical science to be learned, the supply of information in the form of books and of experimental material in every form being inexhaustible.

Thus the first week found Tholfsen and Mrs. Roberts scouring the line of the New York Central for a locomotive in running order. After numerous failures they succeeded in getting the thing going only to discover that the line was blocked with wrecks, and that they would need a crane to clear the track for an exploring journey of even moderate length.

At the same time Murray Lee, with Dangerfield and two or three others, made an effort to get the Park Central's broadcasting station in operation; a work of some difficulty, since it involved ventures into what were for them unknown fields. Daily they tap-tapped messages to each other on telegraph sets rescued from a Western Union office in preparation for the time when they could get a sending set put together.

But the most ambitious effort and the one that was to have the largest ultimate consequences was the expedition of Farrelly, Gloria and a clothing-store proprietor named Kevitz in quest of naval adventure. After a week's intensive study of marine engines from books the three appropriated a tug from the Battery and set off on a cruise of the harbor.

Half an hour later they were high and dry off Bedloe's Island, gloomily contemplating the prospect of spending their lives there. An attempt to swim while weighted down with three hundred pounds of hardware could end only in failure.

Fortunately the tide came to their rescue and with more daring than judgment they continued their voyage to Governor's Island, where they were lucky enough to find a solitary artilleryman, weak with hunger.

The giant birds, which Beeville had professionally named "Tetrapteryxes", seemed to have vacated the city with the appearance of the colonists. Even the nest Roberts had stumbled on proved deserted when an expedition cautiously revisited the place.

Massey, the artist, had gone off on an artistic jag, painting day and night. One morning he took his canvas to the top of the Daily News building to paint the city at dawn from its weather-observation station.

There was an informal rule that everyone should gather at the Institute at ten in the evening unless otherwise occupied, to report on the day's events.

When the artist had not shown up by dawn of the next day, however, Murray and Gloria went to look for him. As they approached the building Murray noticed that the edge of the weather observation platform was twisted awry.

The roof of the building held nothing but the painting on which he had been working—a half-completed sketch of the city as seen from the tower.

"Where do you s'pose he went?" asked Gloria.

"Don't know but he went in a hurry," replied Murray. "He doesn't care about those paintings much more than he does about his life."

"Maybe he took a tumble," she suggested. "Look, there's his easel and it's busted."

"Yes, and that little chair he totes around—look how it's all twisted out of shape."

"Say—" it was Gloria who spoke. "Do you suppose those birds—the tetra-axes or whatever Beeville calls them . . . ?"

They turned and scanned the sky. The calm blue vault, flecked by the fleecy clouds of summer, gave no hint of doom.

"Nothing to do but go home, I guess," said Murray, "and report another robbery in Prospect Park."

The meeting of the colonists that evening was serious.

"It comes to this, then," said Ben. "These birds are dangerous. I think it's a good idea for us to leave here only in pairs and armed until we're certain the danger is over. In fact, I think it would be a good idea for us all to get some guns and ammunition and do target practice."

The meeting broke up on that note and the members of the colony filed into the room where the supply of arms was stored. Presently they formed an automotive cavalcade through the streets in search of a suitable shooting gallery.

When targets were finally set up in the street under automobile lights the general mechanical inefficiency of the colony revealed itself once more. Gloria Rutherford was a dead shot and the artilleryman from Governor's Island almost as good.

Ben himself and Murray Lee, who had been a National Guardsman, knew at least the mechanism of rifles but the rest could only shut their eyes and pull the trigger with the vaguest of ideas as to where the bullet would go. And, as Ben pointed out after the buildings along the street had been peppered with a large portion of Abercrombie and Fitch's stock of ammunition, the supply was not inexhaustible.

"And what shall we do for weapons then?" he asked.

Yoshio, the little Japanese, raised his hand for attention. "I have slight suggestion, perhaps not worthy exalted attention. Why not all people as gentlemen old time in my country, carry sword? It is better than without weapon."

"Why not indeed?" said Ben above a hum of laughter. "Let's go." And an hour later the company re-emerged from an antique store, belted with the strangest collection of swords and kives and fishing gaffs ever borne by an earthly army.

"I wonder, though," said Gloria. "All this hooey doesn't seem to mean much. If those birds are as big as that they aren't going to be scared by these little toad-stabbers."

She was right. That night Ola Mae Roberts was missing.

The siege came a week later, a week during which Murray, with Dangerfield and Tholfsen, worked energetically at their radio and progressed far enough so they could do a fairly competent job of sending and receiving in Morse code. A week during which the naval party got a freighter from the South Street docks and brought her round into the Hudson.

At dawn one morning Gloria, with Farrelly, Kevitz and Yoshio, piled into a limousine with the idea of taking the freighter on a trip to Coney Island. Murray accompanied them to try communicating with the shore via the ship's wireless.

The day was dark with lowering clouds, which explains why they missed seeing the tetrapteryxes. But for the General Sherman statue they never would have seen them until too late. The general's intervention was purely passive. Murray noticed and called Gloria's attention to the curious expression the misty light gave the bronze face and she looked up—to be recalled to her driving by a yell from Kevitz, announcing the metallic carcass of a policeman squarely in their path.

Gloria twisted the wheel sharply to avoid it. The car skidded on the damp pavement and, reeling crazily, caromed into the iron fence around the statue with a crash. At the same moment an enormous mass of rock struck the place where they should have been, sending a shower of fragments whistling about their ears.

Shaken and dazed by the shock they rolled out of the car. As they did so there came a rush of wild wings, an eldritch scream and Yoshio was snatched into the air before their very eyes.

Kevitz fired first, wildly and at random. Murray steadied himself, dropping his gun across his left forearm, shot cool and straight—but at too great a distance.

They saw nothing but a feather or two floating down from the great four-winged bird as it swung off over Central Park, carrying the little Japanese. They saw him squirm in the thing's grip, trying to get his sword loose—and then, with a rattle of dropped stones around them, more of the birds charged home.

Only Gloria had thought of this and withheld her fire. The others swung round as she shot and in an instant the whole group was a maze of whirling wings, clutching claws, shouts, shots and screams. In twenty seconds it was done.

Gloria and Murray rose, panting and breathless, and looked about. Beside them, two gigantic bird-forms were spilling their lives in convulsive agony. Dangerfield and Farrelly were gone.

"What's the next step?" asked Murray with such owlish solemnity that Gloria gave a burst of half-hysterical laughter. She looked around. "Beat it for that building," she said and, gathering her torn skirts about her, set the example.

They made it by the narrowest of margins, standing breathless in what had been the Peacock Alley of one of New York's finest hotels, to see one of the great birds strut past the door.

They waited all day, taking tentative glances from one or another of the windows. The birds remained invisible, apparently not caring for the prospect of a battle in the constricted space of the hotel rooms. But amid the rain and low-hung clouds they might be lurking just outside and both Murray and Gloria judged it too dangerous to venture a dash. As night came on, however, they made a try for the hotel's garage, achieved it without accident and between them rolled one of the cars to the door.

"Wait," said Murray, as Gloria got in. "What was that?"

"This stinking starter." She stirred her foot vigorously. "It won't work."

"No—wait." He held out a restraining hand. A sudden gust of wind bore a dash of rain down against them and with it, from the northeast, a faraway scream, then a tapping and a heavy thud.

"Hot dog!" ejaculated Murray. "They're getting after the crowd. And at night too."

The car jerked forward suddenly as the starter caught. "Hold it," cried Murray. "Douse those headlights." They dodged the wreck of a bus, swung round a corner and headed for First Avenue, gathering speed. Another corner, taken on two wheels in the darkness, the way to the Institute lay before them.

Suddenly a great flame of light sprang out in the sky. There was a crash of rifle fire from window and door of the building and across the front of it one of the birds coasted past. Crash! In the street before them something like a bomb burst, vomiting pennons of fire.

Gloria swung the wheel, swung it back; they had a mad glimpse of brilliantly burning flames inside one of the buildings across the street from the Institute. Then they were tumbling out of the car with rifle fire beating all around them and the thud of dropping objects on either side.

Murray stumbled, but the door was flung open and they were jerked in just as one of the huge bird forms flung itself down past them.

"Thank God, you're safe," said Ben Ruby's voice. "They got Dearborn and Harris and they're besieging us here." He pointed out of the window across the street, where the fire was engulfing the building.

"Did the birds do that little trick?" asked Gloria.

"I hope to tell you, sister. You ain't seen nothing yet, either. They're shedding incendiary bombs all over the shop. How about Kevitz and Farrelly?"

"Got them, too. At the Plaza—and the Japanese. Too bad—I liked that little sprout."

"I thank gracious lady for kindly expressed sentiment, but oversized avians have not yet removed me," said a voice and Gloria looked down to see Yoshio bowing at her side.

"Why how did they come to let you off? Last I saw you were doing a headspin over Central Park."

"I was fortunate. Removing sword I operate on said bird to such extent that he drop me as hot customer, plosh in large tree. To get home is not so easy but I remember armored car provided by intelligent corporation for transport of bankroll, so here I am."

"Bright boy," said Gloria. "Listen!" Above their heads came another crash and shouts. Roberts dashed into the room, rifle in hand. "They've set the place on fire," he said. "We'll have to clear out."

Ben Ruby fumbled at his waist, drew forth a whistle and blew a piercing blast, which was answered by shouts as members of the colony began to pour into the room from various points.

Another bomb burst in a fluff of light just outside the window, throwing weird shadows across the gathering and splitting a pane here and there by the force of its impact.

"Hot stuff," remarked Gloria. "What are they trying to do—take us all at one gulp?"

"Beeville says they're not smart enough. He thinks somebody doesn't like us and is sending them around to tell us so. Listen, everybody!"

The room quieted down.

"We've got to go at once. Our destination is the Times Square subway station. They can't get us there. We'll go in groups of three to a car—one to carry a gun, one a sword and one a light. Everybody got it? Good. Somebody give Gloria one of those express rifles. Here's the list then. First party—Miss Rutherford, gun; Yoshio, sword; O'Hara, light. Go ahead."

With quick handshakes the three made ready. A volley from the windows flashed out and they dashed off. Those inside caught a glimpse of the dark form of their car as it rolled into the night. They were safe at all events.

The second carload, in Yoshio's armored vehicle, also got free; but the third had hardly made half the distance to the parked cars before there was a whir of wings, a scream, the quick burst of a bomb, luckily too far behind them to do damage.

Those inside saw the light-man stop suddenly, flashing his beam aloft, saw an orange flame spring from the gun and then their view of the three was blotted out in a whirl of wings and action.

"Everybody out!" yelled Ben. "Now, while they're busy."

Nobody could remember clearly what did happen. Someone was down—hurt somewhere—but was flung into a car. Through the turmoil the tossing form of one badly-wounded bird struggled on the ground and with a roar of motors the cavalcade started.

Six

It would be futile—and impossible—to chronicle the events of that wild ride. Dawn found them, a depressed group of fourteen, gathered in the protection of the underground passages.

"Well, what next?" asked Gloria. "Do we stay here till they come for us or do we go get 'em?"

"We get out," said Ben. "No good here. They know too much for us."

"Right," declared Beeville. "These birds are intelligent and have some bigger intelligence backing them."

"You mean they'll try to bomb us out of here?" asked Roberts.

McAllister looked up from the dice he was throwing. "You bet your sweet life they will. Those babies know their stuff."

"That's nice," said Gloria, "but what are we going to do about it?"

"Get an anti-aircraft gun from the Island and shell heck out of them when they come round again," suggested the artilleryman.

"Said gun would be considerable weight for individual to transport in pocket," commented Yoshio.

"There's a good deal in that idea," Ben said, "but I don't think it will do as it stands. The birds would bomb our gun to blazes after they had a dose or two from it. They're not so slow, you know. How about some of the forts? Aren't there some big ones around New York?"

McAllister nodded. "There's Hancock. We could get a ship through."

"Say!" Gloria leaped suddenly to her feet. "While we're about it can't we get a battleship or something? There's all kinds of anti-aircraft guns on them."

"There's a destroyer in the Hudson," said someone.

"How many men does it take to run her?"

"Hundred and fifty."

"But," put in Gloria, "that's a hundred and fifty of the old-style men who had to have their three squares and eight hours' sleep every day and they did a lot of things like cooking that we won't have to. What do you say, Dictator, old scout?"

"Okay—unless somebody has something better to offer," declared Ben. In fifteen minutes more the colonists were cautiously en route to take command of U. S. S. *Ward*.

Cleaning up the ship before the start took the colonists a whole day. A sooty dust like the product of a particularly obnoxious factory had settled over everything, and dealing with the cast-iron bodies of the sailors, wedged in the queer corners where they had fallen, was a job in itself.

As night shut down, the whole crew, with the exception of Beeville and Murray Lee, who had spent some time in small boats and had therefore been appointed navigators, was busy going over the engineroom, striving to learn the complex details of handling a warship.

Murray and Beeville were poring over their navigating charts when a step sounded outside the chartroom and the wire-frizzled head of Gloria was thrust in. "How goes it? Do we sail for the Cannibal Islands at dawn?"

"Not on your life," replied Murray. "This hooker is going to pull in at the nearest garage until we learn what it's all about. Talk about arithmetic! This is worse than figuring out a time-table."

Gloria laughed, then her face became serious. "Do you think they'll bomb us again, Mr. Beeville?"

"I don't see why not. They were clear winners in the last battle. But what gets me is where they come from. Why, they're a living refutation of the laws of evolution on the earth! Four wings and two legs!

Bang! The anti-aircraft gun had gone off just outside. With a common impulse the three made for the door and looked upward to see the shell burst in a puff of white clouds of evening, while above and beyond it sailed a black dot with whirring wings.

"That settles it," said Murray. "Whether we like it or not we're going away from here. I wish those nuts hadn't fired though. Now the birds know what we've got. Trot down and tell them to get up steam, that's a good girl, Gloria."

The lone tetrapteryx seemed no more than a scout. But it takes time to get steam up on long disused marine engines and all hands were below when the real attack came.

It began with the explosion of a bomb somewhere outside and a dash of water against the vessel's side that threw all of them off their feet. There was a clang of metal and a rush for the deck —cut across by Ben's voice.

"Take it easy! Everybody to the engines but McAllister, O'Hara and the navigators."

The four sprang for the ladder, Murray in the lead. *Crash!* A sound like the thunder of a thousand tons of scrap iron on a sidewalk and the destroyer pitched wildly.

Murray's head came level with the deck. Instead of the darkness he had expected it was flung into dazzling illumination by a flare burning on the water not fifty yards away, a light so intense that it seemed to have physical body. There was a perceptible wave of heat from it and the water around it boiled like a cauldron.

He tumbled onto the deck, running forward to trip the release of the anchor chain. At the break of the forecastle he stumbled and the stumble saved him, for at that moment another of the bombs fell just in front of the foredeck. The whole bow of the ship seemed to burst into intense, eye-searing flame. Deafened and blinded Murray lay face down on the deck, trying to recover his senses. Behind him the others, equally overwhelmed, tumbled on the iron surface.

But the birds, apparently unaware of how heavy a blow they had struck, seemed wary of the gun. The four heard scream and answering scream above them as the monsters discussed the question on the wing.

If they reached a decision it was too late, for McAllister and O'Hara staggered to the gun and sent a shot shrieking at wild venture into the heavens. Beeville, nearer to the blinding blaze of light, recovered more slowly but found his way to the bridge where he fumblingly pulled the engine-room telegraph over to *Full Speed Ahead*.

Below, in the bowels of the vessel, there was a rumble of activity. A rapid whoosh of steam came from an exhaust pipe, a dash of sparks from the destroyer's funnels and slowly and haltingly she began to move. *Bang!* went the anti-aircraft gun. Beeville heard Murray climbing the bridge behind him and then his cry, "The anchor!"

Too late—with a surge that chanted to a rattle, the destroyer moved, tearing the anchor from its ground and swinging slowly halfway around as the weight dragged the damaged bow to one side. At that moment came another bomb which, but for their motion, would have struck fair and square amidships. *Bang!*

Bang! went the anti-aircraft gun.

Murray dragged at the wheel, then swung the engine-room telegraph back to *Stop*. Just in time—the destroyer's bottom grated on something, her prow rent the side of a big speedboat and she came to rest, pointing diagonally upstream.

Fortunately the attack broke off as rapidly as it had begun. A few screams, lost in the darkness of the night, were the only answer to another shell from the gun. But there was no assurance that this was more than a temporary respite.

Murray and Beeville strove desperately to bring the warped bridge mechanism into running order while O'Hara routed out a blow-torch from somewhere and attacked the chain, now welded into the solid mass of the deck by the force of the light-bomb.

Finally, weaving to and fro in the hands of the inexperienced mariners, she was got round and pointed downstream and out to sea.

Day found them stumbling down the Jersey coast, the fore-deck a mass of wreckage, the ship leaking badly.

"Well, where are we now?" called a cheerful voice, as Murray Lee stood at the wheel. "Australia in sight yet?"

He looked up to see Gloria's head emerging from the companion.

"Come on up," he said, "I'm just going to turn the wheel over to Beeville and get busy with this radio. Don't think the bomb knocked it out. It did everything else though. Look at that."

He indicated the prow, where the fore-turret guns hung like a tired candle and the whole stern of the vessel had dissolved into tears of metal.

"Golly," said Gloria, "that was some egg those birds laid. What was it, anyway?"

"Don't know. Never saw anything like it before. Must be

some kind of new-fangled high-power incendiary bomb to melt steel down like butter. Why, even thermite wouldn't do that. At least, they don't have atomics."

"I hope our friends don't think of looking us up here or we'll be finding out what it's like to walk under water."

"You said something, sister. Wait! I think it got something." He fumbled with the radio dials before him, swinging them this way and that, then clamped on the headset. "Oh, boy, there's something coming through . . . We're not alone in the world then . . . Yes, there she is . . . I wish they wouldn't send so fast . . . AAM Two calling . . . Now who is AAM Two?" His fingers pressed the key in reply as the others watched him with bated breath.

"Position, seventy-three, fifty-three, west longitude; forty, o-three, north latitude. Here"—he wrote the figures down— "take this, one of you and dope it out. Ssh, there's more. Oh, he wants to know who we are and where. Call Ben, Gloria."

She dashed off to return with the dictator just as Beeville, who had been fumbling over the charts with one hand, called suddenly, "Why the position they give is right near here— hardly a hundred miles away. I don't know just what ours is but it can't be far from this spot. Tell them that."

"Find out who they are first," Ben put in. "After what they've done I wouldn't put it past the tetrapteryxes to handle a radio set."

". . . His Majesty's Australian ship *Brisbane*, they say," said Murray. "Wait a minute, since they're so near, I think I can switch them over to the radiophone." He ticked the key a moment, then twisted more dials and leaned back as a full and fruity voice, with a strong English accent, filled the room.

"Compliments of Captain Entwhistle of the Royal Australian Navy to the commander of the U. S. S. *Ward* and can we arrange a meeting? The comet appears to have done a good deal of damage in your part of the world and you are the first people we have encountered."

"Where's your microphone?" asked Ben. "Oh, there—compliments of Benjamin Franklin Ruby, temporarily in command of U. S. S. *Ward* to Captain Entwhistle of the Royal Australian Navy and none of us are sailors. We just borrowed this ship and if you want to see us you'll have to pick us up. We'll keep along the coast toward Cape May. Can you meet us?"

A chuckle came from the radiophone. "I think we can manage it. Are there any of the big birds about in your part of the world? They have been bothering us all summer."

"Yes, that's what we're running away from. They've got some bombs that are pure poison and they've been making regular war on us—probably you know about it?"

"We haven't seen anything like that yet," declared the voice, "but we've had plenty of trouble with them. Hold on a moment. Our lookout reports sighting smoke from your funnels. Hold your course and speed. We'll pick you up."

The voice ceased with a snap and the four in the control room of the destroyer looked at each other.

"I'm glad he came around," remarked Ben. "This destroyer is getting shopworn."

They ceased speaking as the thin pennon of smoke, followed by two tall masts, became visible over the horizon. In a few minutes more the *Brisbane* swept up, swung a circle and came to rest near them, while from her side dropped a barge that began to cut water toward them.

A moment later she was alongside. Ben stepped out on the deck, and as he did so, there was a mutual exclamation of horrified amazement—for Captain Entwhistle of the Royal Australian Navy was as much flesh and blood as any man they had seen in the old days—but a pale blue in color. All his sailors were of the same extraordinary hue.

Seven

There was a moment's silence as the Australian captain steadied himself, staring incredulously at the group that gathered around him.

"Are you—human?" he finally managed to gasp.

"If we aren't somebody's been kidding us," said Gloria. "But are you? You're all blue!"

"Of course," said the captain. "It was the comet. We knew it struck in America somewhere but didn't know where, or what it did. What's the matter with your ship?" He indicated the wrecked and leaking bow. "She seems to . . . ___ by the head."

"Oh, that was a valentine from the birds, ___ ___ u. . . you give us quarters on your vessel? There aren't many of us."

"Of course, of course. Come on. We can discuss things better in my cabin."

As they mounted to the deck of the *Brisbane* even the trained sailors, the light blue of their faces oddly at variance with the dark blue of their uniforms, could not refrain from staring at the colonists. They crowded into the captain's cabin past rows of eager blue faces.

"I suggest," said Captain Entwhistle, "that we begin by telling each other how this happened. I can scarcely credit the fact that you are human and can walk and talk. Would any of you care for a whisky and soda?"

"No, thanks," said Murray, "but I'll have a drink of lubricating oil if you can find any."

The naval officer looked at him and remarked, a trifle stiffly, "Certainly, if you wish. Williams . . ."

"Oh, don't mind him," Ben Ruby cut in. "Pardon me, Captain, he can drink lubricating oil perfectly well but he's joking with you. You were saying about the comet . . ."

"Why, you knew that the big comet struck earth as predicted, didn't you? It was on the morning of February sixteenth, last year—evening of February fifteenth by American time. Even in our country, which is on the other side of the earth, it caused a good deal of damage. The gases it set free put everybody to sleep and caused a lot of wreckage.

"Our scientists say the gases of the comet in some unexplained way altered the iron in the haemoglobin of our blood to cobalt. It seems to work just as well but that's why we're all blue. I don't quite understand it myself but you know how these medical Johnnies are. Now what happened to you people?"

"May I ask something first?" said Beeville. "What day is this?"

"August eighteenth, nineteen sixty-two."

"Good Lord! Then we were there for over a year!"

"Yes," said Ben. "All of us returned to consciousness about the same time two months ago. We know nothing of what the comet did to us, or how this change occurred, except that when we woke up we were just what you see.

"All we know is that we're composed of metal that doesn't rust easily, make our meals off electricity and find the taste of any kind of oil agreeable. And the birds . . ." He broke off with a gesture.

"Oh yes, the birds," said the captain. "Have they been annoying you too? That's one of the reasons why we're here. I assume you mean the big four-winged birds we call dodos down under.

"We haven't seen much of them but occasionally they come and fly away with a sheep or even a man. One of our aviators chased one several hundred miles out to sea recently and we had assumed they came from one of the islands. Our scientists don't know what to make of them."

"Neither do ours except that they're an unadulterated brand of hell," put in Murray. "We were all living in New York, snug as bugs in a rug, when they began dropping incendiary bombs on us and carrying off anyone they could get hold of."

"Including this insignificant person," said Yoshio, proudly.

"Incendiary bombs! Do you mean to tell me they have intelligence enough for that?"

"I'll say they have! Did you see the prow of our ship? That's where one of their little presents got home. If you really want to find out what it's all about come on up to New York—but get ready for the fight of your life."

The captain leaned back, sipping his drink meditatively. "Do you know," he said, "that's just what I was thinking of doing? Frankly your story is all but incredible but here you are as proof of it and you don't seem to be robots except in appearance."

"Oh, boy!" whispered Murray to Gloria. "Wait till these babies get after the birds with their eight-inch guns. They'll wish they'd never heard of us."

"Well, I'm willing to try an attack, or at least a reconnaissance of them," said the captain. "Just now we're in the position of an armed exploring party.

"After the comet struck, all the cables went dead. We got into radio communication with the Dutch colonial stations at Baravia and later with South Africa, but the rest of the world is just being re-explored and my commission authorizes me to resist unfriendly acts. I think you could call an incendiary bomb an unfriendly act."

His eyes twinkled over this mild witticism and the party broke up with a scraping of chairs. A couple of hours later the blue line of Sandy Hook was visible, then the vague cliffs of the New York skyscrapers.

Of the tetrapteryxes or "dodos" as the Australian had called them there was no sign. Murray Lee felt someone stir at his side and looked round.

"Oh, blast!" said Gloria Rutherford. "It's so beautiful that I want to cry. Did you ever feel like that?"

He nodded silently. "And those birds—isn't it a shame somehow that they should have the most beautiful city in the world?"

The shrill of a whistle cut off his words. With marvelous, machine-like precision, the sailors moved about the decks. The *Brisbane* lost way, came to a halt and there was a rush of steel as the anchor ran out. Captain Entwhistle came down from the bridge.

"I don't see anything of your dodos yet," he said. "Do you think it would be wise to send out a landing party, Mr. Ruby?"

"Most certainly not," said Ben. "You don't know what you're up against yet. Wait till they come around. You'll have plenty to do."

The captain shrugged. Evidently he was not at all unwilling to match the Australian navy against anything the dodos might do. "Very well, I'll accept your advice for the present, Mr. Ruby. It is near evening in any case. But if there is no sign of them in the morning I propose to land and look over the city."

In the middle of the night as Ben, Murray and Gloria were seated in the chartroom of the ship, chatting with the young lieutenant on duty there, there came a quick patter of feet on the deck, and a shout of "Light, ho!"

"There are your friends now, I'll wager," said the lieutenant. "Now watch us go get 'em. If you want to see the fun better go up on the bridge. All we do here is wrestle slide-rules."

Hastily the three climbed the bridge, where a little group of officers were clustered. Following the direction in which they were looking they saw, just above the buildings on the Jersey shore, what looked like a tall electric sign, burning high in the air and some distance away with no visible means of support.

"What do you make of it?" asked Captain Entwhistle, turning and thrusting a pair of glasses into Ben's hands. Through them he could read the letters.

SOFT MEN EXIT. HARD MEN ARE WORKERS BE-
LONGING. MUST RETURN. THIS MEANS YOU.

"Looks like a dumb joke by someone who doesn't know English very well," he opined, passing the glasses to Gloria.

"Wait a minute though," said Gloria as she read the letters. "Remember they caught Dangerfield and Farrelly and the rest. Maybe *they* taught them how to speak."

"Yes, but those two didn't know anything about 'soft men.' And what do they mean by 'belonging'?"

"Look, sir," said one of the younger officers, "it's changing."

Abruptly the lights were blotted out, to reappear amid a swimming of colors, nearer and larger.

WARNING, they read this time, FLY AWAY ACCURSED PLACE.

"What beats me," said Ben, "is what makes that light. How do they do it?"

"Well, we'll find out," said the Captain. "Mr. Sturgis, switch on searchlights three and four and turn them on the source of that light."

A few quick orders and two long beams of light leaped out from the ship toward the source of the mysterious sky-writing —leaped but not fast enough. For even as the searchlights sought for their goal the lights were extinguished.

Gloria shivered. "I think I want to go away from this place," she said. "There's too much we don't know about around here."

"Apparently someone wants us to clear out," said Captain Entwhistle. "Mr. Sturgis, get steam on three boilers and send the men to reserve action stations. We may have something doing here before morning."

Orders were shouted, iron doors slammed and feet pattered in the interior of the warship. From their station on the bridge Ben, Gloria and Murray could see the long shafts of the turret guns swing upward to their steepest angle, then turn toward the Jersey shore. The *Brisbane* was preparing for emergencies.

But there was no fight that night.

At four o'clock Captain Entwhistle retired, reappearing at eight, fresh as though he had slept through the whole night. The colonists, while the sailors stared at them, submitted themselves to an electric meal from one of the ship's dynamos.

Morning found them gathering about the upper decks, eager for action, particularly McAllister, who had spent most of the night engaged in highly technical discussions of the *Brisbane's* artillery with one of the turret-captains.

"What do you suggest?" asked the captain. "Shall we land a party?"

"I hate to go without taking a poke at those birds," said Ben, "but still I don't think it would be safe."

"What's the matter with that plane?" asked Gloria.

The captain looked at Ben. "There may be something in that idea. I'll let you or one of your people go as an observer."

"Tickled to death," Ben replied. "We never got beyond the upper part of the city ourselves. The dodos were too dangerous. I'd like to find out what it's all about."

"How about me?" offered Gloria.

"Nothing doing, kid. You get left this time. If those birds get after us we may land in the bay with a bump and I don't want this party to lose its little sunshine."

"Up anchor!" came the command. "Revolutions for ten knots speed. I'm going to head down the bay," he explained. "If anything happens I want to have searoom, particularly if they try bombing us."

Fifteen minutes later, with the *Brisbane* running into the morning land-breeze in an ocean smooth as glass, Ben and the pilot—a lad whose cheeks must have been rosy before the comet but were now a vivid blue—were in the air.

Beneath them the panorama of New York harbor lay spread. As they ro-- Ben could make out the line of the river, shining through the pearly haze like a silver ribbon.

The towers of the city tilted, then swung toward them as the pilot swept down nearer for an examination. Everything seemed normal save at the north and east, where a faint smoky mist still lingered over the buildings they had occupied. Of birds or of other human occupation than their own there was no sign.

"What do you say, old chap?" asked the pilot. "What direction shall we explore?"

"Let's go up the Hudson," Ben suggested. "They seemed to come from that direction."

"Check." They climbed, swung and went on. They were over Yonkers. Ben could see a river steamer at the dock, where she had made her last halt.

"Throw in that switch marked RF. That's for communicating with the ship."

"Okay," said Ben. "Hello. . . . Yes, this is Ruby in the plane. Nothing to report. Everything serene. We're going to explore further up the river."

In the distance the Catskills loomed before them, blue and proud. Ben felt a touch on his back and looked round. "What's that off on the left—right in the mountains? No, there."

Following the indicated direction Ben saw something like a scar on the projecting hillside—not one of the ancient rocks but a fresh cut on the earth as though a wide spot had been denuded of vegetation.

"I don't know. Never saw it before. Shall we go see? . . . Hello, *Brisbane*. Ruby reporting. There is a mysterious clearing in the Catskills. We are investigating."

Eight

The bare area seemed to run all down a long valley and spread out as it rounded the crest of a hill which hid what lay behind it from their view. As they watched a gray speck lumbered slowly down the valley. Then Ben noticed a tiny flicker of red light, so bright as to be clearly visible even in the day, where the grey speck moved against the hillside. A door seemed to open in the hillside.

Focusing the glasses the pilot handed him he could just make out a square bulky object that trundled forth. And then one—two—three—four—five of the huge dodo-tetrapteryx birds shot out, poised for a moment, leaped into flight.

"Hello, *Brisbane*," called Ben. "Five dodos have taken off from the cutting in the hills. I think they are after us. Better turn back this way and get ready for trouble."

The pilot had turned the plane. Ben swung round to look over his shoulder. The dodos were already some yards in the air. Behind them the bulky object was running slowly out of the opening in the hillside. It had the appearance of a very long flexible cannon. As he held his glasses on it it stopped, straightened out and the muzzle was elevated in their direction.

"*Dive!*" he shouted suddenly into the voice tube, entirely on impulse.

The plane banked sharply and seemed to drop straight down. At the same instant, right through the spot where they had just passed, shot a beam of light so brilliant that it outshone the morning sun. There was a roar louder than that of the motor. The plane pitched and heaved and the lightbeam went off as suddenly as it had snapped on.

"Didn't I tell you those babies were posion?" he remarked. "Boy, if that ever hit us!"

"What was it?"

"Don't know but it was something terrible. Let's head for home and momma. I don't care about this."

The plane reeled as the pilot handled the controls. The lightbeam shot out again, just to one side this time. Out of the corner of his eye Ben could see one of the birds—gaining on them!

"How do you work this machinegun?" he asked.

"Just squeeze the trigger. Look *out!* I'm going to dive her again."

With a roar the light-beam let go a third time. Ben saw the edge of it graze their right wingtip. The plane swung wildly round and down, the pilot fighting for control.

The earth seemed to rush up to meet them, tumbling, topsy-turvy. Ben noted a warped black spot where the beam had touched the wingtip, then, surprisingly, they were flying along, level with the surface of the Hudson beneath them and hardly a hundred feet up.

"That was close," came the pilot's voice, shaky with relief. "I thought they had us that time. That's quite a ray they have."

"It sure is one first-class heller," agreed Ben. "Are you far enough down to duck it now?"

"I think so unless they can put it through the hills or chase us with it. Do you suppose those dodos thought that up themselves?"

"Can't tell. They're right on their toes though." He pointed up and back. Silhouetted against the sky they could see three of them, flying in formation. "Can we make it?"

"I'm giving the old bus all she'll stand. The *Brisbane* will come toward us though. Wait till those guys get going. They'll find we can take a trick or two."

Yonkers again. Ben looked anxiously over his shoulder. The three silhouettes were a trifle nearer. One Hundred Twenty-fifth Street and the long bridge swung into view, then Riverside Drive and the procession of docks with the rusting liners lying beside them.

Ben waggled the machine-gun, and squeezed the trigger. A little line of smoke-puffs leaped forth. Tracer bullets—but nowhere near the birds. On and on—lower New York—the Battery.

Wham! The water beneath and behind them boiled. Ben looked up. The birds were above them, too high to be reached, dropping bombs.

"All right, old soaks," he muttered, "keep that up. You'll never hit us that way."

Again something struck the water beneath them. The plane pitched and swerved as the pilot changed course to disturb the aim of the bombers. In the distance the crusier could be seen now, heading toward them. As he watched there was a flash from her foredeck. Up in the blue above them appeared the white burst of a shell, then another.

One of the dodos suddenly dived out of the formation, sweeping down more swiftly than Ben would have believed possible. He swung the gun this way and that, sending out streams of tracers, but the bird did not appear to heed.

Closer—closer—and then with a crash something burst right

behind him. The plane gyrated—the water rushed upward. The end he thought, and wondered whether his teeth would rust. The next moment the water struck them.

When Ben Ruby came to, he beheld a ceiling which moved jerkily to and fro and stared lazily at it, wondering what it was. Then memory returned with a snap. He sat up and looked about him. He was in one of those cubbyholes which are called cabins on warships, alone.

Beneath him he could hear the steady throb of the engines. At his side was a small table with a wooden rack on it. In one compartment stood a glass, whose contents proved to be oil. He drank it, looked at and felt of himself. Finding nothing wrong he got out of the hammock and stepped to the door. A seaman was on guard in the corridor.

"Where is everybody?"

"On deck, sir. I hope you are feeling all right now, sir."

"Top of the world, thanks. Is the pilot okay?"

"Yes, sir. This way."

He ascended to the bridge, to be greeted riotously by the assembled company. The *Brisbane* was steaming steadily along in the open sea with no speck of land in sight and no traces of the giant birds.

"What happened?" Ben asked. "Did you get rid of 'em?"

"I think so. We shot down two and the rest made off after trying to bomb us. What did you find out?"

Ben briefly described their experiences. "I thought there was something wrong with one of your wingtips," said the captain, "but your plane sank so quickly after being hit that we didn't have time to examine it. That light-ray cannon of theirs sounds serious. Do you suppose the dodos managed it?"

"Can't tell," said Ben. "From what I could make out though, it didn't look like birds that were handling it."

"But what could they be?"

"*Ask* me! Delirium tremens, I guess. Nothing in this world is what it ought to be any more. Where did those birds come from—how did we get this way, all of us—who is it up there in the Catskills that don't like us? Answer me those and I'll tell you who was handling the gun."

"Message, sir," said a sailor, touching his cap and offering a folded paper. The captain read it.

"There you are." He extended the sheet to Ben. "My government is recalling all ships. Our sistership, the *Melbourne*, has been attacked off San Francisco and severely damaged by bomb-dropping dodos and they have made a mass descent on Sumatra. Gentlemen, this has all the characteristics of a formal war."

"If you were not before my eyes," said Sir George Graham Harris, president of the Australian Scientific Commission, "as proof of what you say, and if our biological and metallurgical experts did not report that your physiology is utterly beyond their comprehension, I would believe you were Robots.

"However, that is not the point. I have here a series of reports from different quarters on such explorations as have been made since the arrival of the comet and our recovery from its effects. We are, it appears, confronted with a menace of considerable gravity in the form of these birds.

"In the light of your closer acquaintance with them and with conditions generally in the devastated areas they may be more suggestive to you than to us." He stopped and ruffled over the papers piled beside him at the big conference table.

He was a kindly old gentleman, whose white Van Dyke and pale blue lips contrasted oddly with the almost indigo tint of his visage. Smiling round the table at his scientific colleagues and at Ben, Murray, Gloria and Beeville, who occupied the positions of honor, he went on.

"I give you excerpts. The first is from the South African government. They have—hm, hm—sent an aerial expedition northward, all lines of communication appearing to be broken. At Nairobi, they report for the first time, finding a town entirely unoccupied and its inhabitants turned into cast-metal statues.

"Addis Ababa the same—Wadi Hafa likewise. Twenty miles north of Wadi Hafa they noted the first sign of life—a bird of some kind at a considerable distance to the west of them and flying parallel with them and very rapidly."

The scientist looked up. "It would appear beyond doubt that this bird belonged to the species to which Dr. Beeville has given the excellent scientific name, tetrapteryx.

"As the expedition proceeded northward, they encountered more of them—sometimes as many as four being in sight at one time. At Alexandria, where they halted for supplies, the dodos closed in. When the expedition took to the air again with the object of flying to Crete and thence to Europe these avians came very close, apparently trying to turn the expedition back.

"They reached Crete that afternoon in spite of the interference of the birds, but that night were attacked on the ground. The phenomena that accompanied all other attacks were observed. The birds used incendiary bombs of great intensity. One machine was entirely destroyed. The others, since their object was exploration, at once took to the air and returned.

"Any comments, gentlemen? No? Well, the next is the report of the Dutch ship *Corlaer*, which attempted to reach Japan. She was permitted to proceed to within a few miles of the islands and then began to receive light-warnings in the sky such as Captain Entwhistle reports. Unfortunately they were in Japanese characters and there was no one aboard who could read them.

"She put in at the port of Nagasaki and sent out a landing

party. It never returned. As in the other cases the ship was bombed at night and only made Sumatra with the greatest difficulty.

"There are minor reports with which I will not bother you. But the report of H.M.A.S. *Melbourne* appears highly significant. She touched at several South American ports. In the cities she reports finding all life at a standstill, although at Iquique the landing party encountered some hill-Indians who had suffered a bluing of the blood similar to ours and who proved distinctly unfriendly. They are reported as engaged in looting the city and getting drunk on the contents of the bodegas.

"North of Callao she found no signs of life until she reached San Pedro Bay. There a man was observed to be waving from the beach. The *Melbourne* put in and launched a boat. Before it reached shore one of the birds made its appearance overhead and the man disappeared and was not seen again.

"Shortly afterward, the *Melbourne* began to see the dodos constantly and at the region of San Francisco she saw one of the light signals. The wording of it was DEPART AWAY FAREWELL FOREVER."

Gloria stirred and Sir George looked at her. "Nothing, sir. I was just thinking that these dodos are uncommonly poetical. They told us to fly from the accursed place."

"Yes, yes. Naturally the *Melbourne*, not anticipating any trouble as the result of a refusal to obey this absurd command, steamed into the bay. Like the other ships she was attacked at night. One of the bombs fell on the fire-control station and wrecked it, bringing down the tripod mast and fusing the top of the conning tower.

"She got under way immediately and replied with all guns but before escaping number three turret was struck by another bomb and all the men in the turret were killed. The roof of the turret was driven in and even the breeches of the guns melted.

"That, I think, summarizes the reports we have. We have seen a few of the birds, mostly at a distance, and they appear to have carried off several individuals, especially in Sumatra. I am afraid that is all we can offer."

There was a moment's silence.

"Well, what the material in the bombs is I can't say," said Ben, "but they know all about projecting it from guns in the form of a beam."

"The eggs Roberts found too," said Gloria.

"Oh yes, Dr. Beeville can tell you about that."

"Why, there's nothing much to it. One of our people found what appeared to be a nest of these birds in a building. The nest was built of soft cloths and contained large eggs but when the place was revisted the eggs had been removed.

"I may say that I have examined the remains of one rather badly mangled specimen. The brain-case is extraordinarily large

—larger than I have ever seen in any animal—and they appear to be of a high order of intelligence.

"They do not appear to wish to destroy us mechanical men but to carry us off. The messages seen by the ships seem to indicate that the intelligence behind these birds is capable of reading and understanding English. I cannot conceive that the birds themselves would be able to do this.

"Further, there is the evidence of the gun which fired on Mr. Ruby. In every case where these birds have attacked man, they have used bombs of this material put up in portable form, although the gun would have been much more effective. It would have gone right through the *Melbourne* or the *Brisbane* like a red-hot poker through a board.

"From this I argue that the birds are directed rather than directing and that the directing intelligence is eigher too indolent or too contemptuous of us to attack man except through their agency. I deduce that we are dealing with some powerful and as yet unknown form of life. What it is or how it reached the earth I am not prepared to say."

"Wunnerful," said Gloria irreverently, and a smile passed across the faces of the conferees.

"But what are the bombs made of and what makes them tick?" asked Murray Lee.

"That is a question to which I would very much like to know the answer," said Sir George, stroking his white beard. "Perhaps Mr. Nasmith, our chemical member, will be good enough to give us something on the point."

"Not much," said Nasmith, a lantern-jawed man. "We made a chemical analysis of the portions of the *Melbourne* which were struck by the bombs and all we can say is that it gave a most extraordinary result. These portions were originally made of Krupp armor steel as you know. Our analysis showed the presence of a long series of chemical elements, including even gold and thorium, most of them in minute quanities. Titanium appeared to be the leading constituent after iron."

"Then," said Sir George, "the situation appears to be this— we don't know what the dodos are or what is behind them but they have possession of a large part of the world to which they are disposed to forbid us any access.

"They have powerful weapons and they appear to be unfriendly. I suggest that the judgment of this meeting be that the government take immediate measures of investigation and, if necessary, of hostility."

"Swell," said Gloria, "only you didn't go half far enough. We've been there and you haven't. You want to get the best guns you've got and go for them right away."

There was a murmur of approval. As Sir George rose to put the question to a vote there came a knock at the door. Heads were turned to greet a young man who hurried to the president and whispered something. Sir George turned to the meeting with a startled face.

"Ladies and gentlemen," he said, "the dodos are bombing Canberra, the capital of Australia, and are being engaged by the Royal Australian Air Force."

Nine

"I'm glad," said Gloria to Murray Lee as they leaned against the rail of the steamer *Paramatta* in their new American Army uniforms, "that they're going to attack these things in the old U. S. I'd hate like anything to think we last Americans were shoved out of our country by a lot of chickens."

Murray glanced around him. In every direction the long lines of the convoy stretched out, big liners loaded to the funnels with men, guns, tanks and ammunition. On the fringes of the troopships the sleek gray sides of the cruisers and destroyers that protected them were visible. Overhead there soared an armada of fighting planes, which could maneuver better than a dodo.

He nodded.

In the four months since the conference with the Australian Scientific Committee, a carefully-worked out campaign had evidently been set in operation by whatever central intelligence led the four-winged birds with the object of wiping human life from the earth. The bombing of Canberra was merely the first blow.

While Australia was arming and organizing to meet the menace the second blow fell—on Surabaya, the great metropolis of Java, which was wiped out in a single night. There was apparently no life in Europe, and atomic weapons could not be obtained.

When, late in November, a flock of twenty-five dodos was observed over north Australia, headed for Sydney, the forces of the defense were on their guard. Long before the birds reached the town they were met by a desperate battle over the desert, claw and beak and bomb against machine-gun. They were shot down to the last bird. With that the attacks had suddenly ceased.

It was realized that whatever lay behind this attempt to conquer all that was left of the old earth must be in some way due to the coming of the great comet and must center somewhere in America, where the comet had struck.

Delegates from the three surviving governments met in conference at Perth with Ben Ruby accorded a place as the representative of the United States. The decision of the conference was to mobilize every man and weapon to attack the birds in America and exterminate them there if possible. If unable to do this, then to keep them so occupied at home that they would be unable to deliver any counter-attack.

There was plenty of shipping to carry an army far larger than that the federated governments could mobilize. The main weakness of the expedition lay in the lack of naval protection, for the great navies of the world had perished when the northern hemisphere passed under the influence of the comet.

It was sought to make up for this deficiency by a vast cloud of planes, flying from the decks of many merchant ships converted into carriers, though some of the new jets were powerful enough to cruise around the world under their own power.

And so, this March morning in 1963, the armada was crossing the Atlantic toward the United States. In view of the fact that the headquarters of the dodos seemed to be somewhere in the Catskills it had been decided to land in New Jersey, form a base there and work northward.

In the preliminary training for the coming conflict the metal Americans had played an important part. Their construction made them impossible as flyers, which they would have preferred. But quite early it was discovered that they made ideal operators for tanks. The oil fumes and the lack of air did not in the least affect beings to whom breathing had become unimportant and the oil was actually a benefit.

As a result the American army had been composed of fourteen tanks of special type. They were given extra-heavy armor, fitted in two thicknesses, with a chamber between as protection against the light-bombs, and each tank, built to be handled by a single operator, was provided with one heavy gun, so arranged that it could be used against aerial attack.

A stir of motion was visible at the head of the convoy. A destroyer dashed past the *Paramatta*, smoke pouring from her funnels, white bow-wave rising high at her bridge as she put on full speed. From the airplane carrier just behind them in the line, one, two, three flights of fighters swung off, circled a moment to gain altitude, then whirled off to the north and west.

"What is it?" asked Gloria.

A sailor touched his cap. "Sighted a dodo, I believe, miss," he said.

"Oh boy! Here we go."

They craned their necks eagerly but nothing was visible except a few flecks in the sky. Faint and faraway, a rattle of machine-guns drifted down. There was a flash of intense light like the reflection in a far-distant mirror and the machine-guns ceased. A few moments later the planes came winging back to their mother ship. A sailor on her deck began to swing his arms in curious semaphore language of the sea.

"What happened?" asked Gloria of the man by their side.

"I'm trying to make out, miss. One dodo, he says, carrying a bomb—hit—by—machine-gun—oh! The bomb went off in the dodo's claws and blew him all to pieces."

The echo of a cheer came across the water from the other ships.

That night dodos announced their presence by a few bombs dropped tentatively among the ships. They did no damage, and by morning the dream-towers of Atlantic City, flecked by the early morning sun, rose out of the west.

Far in the distance the flyers of the expedition had spied more of the birds but after the first day's encounter with the planes they kept a healthy distance, apparently contented to observe what they could.

As ship after ship swung in toward the piers and discharged its cargo of men, guns and munitions the birds became bolder, as though to inspect what was going on. But the Australian flyers attacked them fiercely, driving them back at every attempt to pierce the aerial umbrella, and when night came on nearly a third of the force had been landed and quartered in parts of the one-time pleasure city.

Covered by the darkness a few dodos came down to drop bombs that night.

The whir of the birds' wings was plainly audible, and before they had realized that man had a weapon to meet their night attacks half a dozen of them had been caught in the bursts of anti-aircraft guns and more had been met and shot down by the night-patrolling airmen.

The next morning saw the unloading beginning anew while the emptied transports were taken around into Delaware Bay. Fortunately the weather continued unusually fine for late March, bright with sunshine, giving the dodos no opportunity to attack behind the cover of clouds. There was just enough cold in the air to make the Australians and South Africans lively, though the Americans found the temperature caused the oil to move sluggishly in their metallic joints.

At daybreak the whole American unit had been pushed out to the railroad line at Greenwood with the advance guard of tanks. Finding no opposition they continued on to Farmington, where there was an airport that would serve for the leading squadrons of planes.

"Do you know," said Ben to Murray, "I wish those dodos would show a little more pep. Fighting them is no cinch. We're a little ahead of the game now but that's because they've let us alone and haven't brought up any of those light-beam guns."

"Maybe we've got 'em on the run," replied Murray.

"Yes, but we've seen enough of these babies to know they haven't got a yellow streak a millimeter wide in their whole make-up. Yet here they let us do just about as we please. Makes me think they're just laying for us and when they get us where they want us—zowie!"

"Mebbe so, mebbe so," replied Murray. "Beeville still thinks they've got a big boss somewhere running the whole works and till we find out what's behind it we're fighting in the dark."

The country between Atlantic City and Philadelphia is flat with a few gentle elevations, dotted with small towns, farms and bits of woodland. In the cold spring morning of the next day, with rain portented, the army of the federated governments pushed out along the roads like a huge many-headed snake, tanks and planes in the lead, steady ranks of infantry and the big guns coming behind.

Back at Atlantic City all machine-shops and factories had been set in operation and wrecking crews were already clearing the railroads and mounting huge long-range guns on trucks, preparatory to covering the advance. All along the route was bustle and hurry. Camp kitchens rumbled along, harassed officers tore up and down the lines in their jeeps and messengers rushed to and fro on popping motorcycles.

Out with the advance the American division of fourteen tanks rolled along. The dodos seemed to have completely disappeared, even the scouting airmen far ahead reporting no sign of them. The army was succeeding in establishing itself on American soil.

But around noon a *stop* signal flashed on the control boards of the tanks. They halted at the crest of a little rise and climbed out to look around.

"What is it?" asked someone.

"Perhaps gentlemanly general wishes to disport in surf," suggested Yoshio, "and proceeding is retained without presence."

"Perhaps," said Gloria. "But I'll bet that the dodos are getting in their licks somewhere."

"Well, we'll soon know," said Murray Lee. "Here comes a dispatch rider."

The man on the motorcycle dashed up, saluted. "General Ruby?" he inquired and handed the dispatch to Ben. The latter read it.

"Well, here it is, folks," he said, "Listen to this—'General Grierson to General Ruby. Our flank guard was heavily attacked at Atsion this morning. The Third Brigade of the Fourteenth Division has suffered heavy casualties and has been forced back to Chew Road. We are bringing up heavy artillery. The enemy appear to be using large numbers of light-ray guns. Advance guard is recalled to Waterford in support of our left flank.' "

"Oh—oh," said somebody.

"I knew they'd start giving us hell sooner or later," remarked Murray Lee as he climbed into his tank.

At Waterford there was ordered confusion when they arrived. Just outside the town a long line of infantrymen were plying pick and shovel in the formation of a system of trenches. Machine-gun units were installing themselves in stone or brick buildings and constructing barricades around their weapons.

Line after line of tanks had wheeled into position under cover of woods or in the streets of the town, light-weights out in front, with their six-inch guns farther back.

Artillery was everywhere, mostly in little pits over which the gunners were spreading green strips of camouflage. As the American tanks rolled up, a battery of eight-inch howitzers behind a railroad embankment at the west end of the town was firing slowly and with an air of great solemnity at some target in the invisible distance, the angle of their muzzles showing that they were using extreme range.

A couple of planes were overhead. But of dead or wounded, of dodos or any other enemy there was no sign. It might have been a parade-war. Guides directed the Americans to a post down the line toward Chew Road.

"What's the news?" asked Ben of an officer whose red tabs showed he belonged to the staff.

"They hit the right wing at Atsion," replied the officer. "Just what happened I'm not sure. Somebody said they had a lot of those light-ray guns and they just crumpled up our flank. We lost about fifteen hundred men in fifteen minutes. Tanks, too. But I think we're stopping them now."

"Any dodos?" asked Ben.

"Just a few. The planes shot down a flock of seven just before the battle and after that they kept away. What is it? General Witherington wants me? Oh, all right, I'll come. Excuse me, sir," and the staff officer was off.

Most of the afternoon was spent in an interminable period of waiting and watching the laboring infantry sink themselves into the ground. About four o'clock a fine cold drizzle began to fall. The Americans sought the shelter of their tanks and their radiophones flashed the order to move up toward the north and east, through a barren pasture with a few trees in it, to the crest of a low hill.

It was already nearly dusk. The tanks bumped unevenly over the stony ground, their drivers following each other by the black silhouettes in the gloom. Off to the right a battery suddenly woke to a fever of activity, then as rapidly became silent. Evidently dodos were abroad in the gloom.

At the crest of the hill they could see across a flat valley in the direction of Chew Road. Something seemed to be burning behind the next rise. A ruddy glare lit the clouds. Down the line guns began to growl again and the earth trembled gently with the sound of an explosion somewhere in the rear.

There were trees along their ridge and, looking through the side peephole of his tank, Murray could make out the vague forms of a line of whippets among them, waiting like themselves for the order to advance. He wondered what the enemy were like. Evidently not all dodos, since so many tanks had been pushed up to the front. This argued a man or animal that ran along the ground. The dodos seemed to spend most of their time in the air.

He was recalled from his meditations by the ringing of the attention bell and the radiophone began to speak rapidly.

"American tank division—enemy tanks reported approaching. Detain them as long as possible and then retire. Your tanks are not to be sacrificed. Radio your positions with reference to Clark Creek as you retire for guidance of artillery registering on enemy tanks. There . . ."

The voice broke off in mid-sentence. So the dodos had tanks! Murray Lee snapped in his controls and glanced forward. Surely in the gloom along that distant ridge there was a darker spot— next to the house—something.

Suddenly, with a roar like a thousand thunders, a bolt of sheer light seemed to leap from the dark shape on the opposite hill, straight toward the trees where Murray had noticed the whippets. He saw one of the trees leap into vivid flame from root to branch as the beam struck it—saw a whippet, sharply outlined in the fierce glow, its front armor-plate caving. Then its ammunition blew up in a shower of sparks and he was frantically busy with his own controls and gun.

Ten

All along the line of the American tanks the guns flamed. Flame-streaked fountains of dirt leaped up around the dark shape on the opposite hill and a burst of fire came from the farmhouse beside it as a misdirected shell struck it somewhere.

The beam from the unknown enemy snapped off suddenly as it had come on, leaving, like lightning, an aching of the eyes behind it. Murray Lee swung his tank round, making for the reverse slope of the hill to avoid the light-beam.

Crack! The beam came on again—right overhead this time. It flashed through the treetops leaving a trail of fire. He heard a torn branch bang on the roof of his tank, manipulated the gun to fire at the square of the beam and discovered that the magazine was empty.

As he bent to snap on the automatic shell-feeding device, a searchlight from somewhere lashed out, then went off. In the second's glimpse it afforded the enemy appeared as a huge, polished fish-shaped object, its mirror-like sides unscarred by the bombardment it had passed through, its prow bearing a long prehensile snout—apparently the source of the light-beam.

Suddenly a shell screamed overhead and the whole scene leaped into dazzling illumination as it burst just between the enemy tanks and their own. It must be a shell from the dodos!

The federated armies had no shells that dissolved into burning light. Then a whole chorus of shells, falling in the village behind them.

Murray had a better look at their opponent in the light. It seemed to lie flush with the ground. There was no visible means of either support or propulsion. It was all of twenty feet in diameter, widest near the head, tapering backward. The questing snout swung to and fro, fixed its position and discharged another of those lightning-bolts.

Off to the right came the answering crash as it caved in the armor of another of the whippets. He aimed his gun carefully at the base of the snout and pulled the trigger. On the side of the monster there appeared a flash of flame as the shell exploded, then a bright smear of metal—a direct hit and not the slightest damage!

Ben Ruby's voice came through the radiophone. "Pull out, folks—our guns are no good against that baby. I'm cutting off. Radio positions back to the heavy artillery. Put the railroad guns on."

Murray glanced through the side peephole again. One, two, three, four, five—all the American tanks seemed undamaged. The monster had confined its attention to the whippets. He pulled his throttle back, shot the speed up, rumbling down the hill, toward the village.

As he looked back, darkness had closed in. The brow of the hill, its rows of trees torn and broken by the light-beam, stood between him and the enemy. Before him, amid the flaring light of the enemy shells, was a stir of movement. The troops seemed to be pulling out also.

The tanks rumbled through the streets of Waterford and came to a halt on a corner behind a stone church which held three machine-gun nests.

A messenger dashed down the street, delivered his missive to someone, and out of the shadows a file of infantry suddenly popped up and began to stream back, getting out of range. Then, surrounded by bursts of artillery fire, illumined by the glare of half a dozen searchlights that flickered restlessly on and off, the strange thing came over the brow of the hill.

It halted for a moment, its snout moving about uneasily as though it were smelling out the way. As it did so, it was joined by a second. Neither of them seemed to be in the least disturbed by the shells all the way from light artillery to six-inch, that were bursting about them, filling the air with singing fragments. For a moment they stood at ease.

Then the left-hand one discharged one of its flaming bolts. It struck squarely in the center of an old brick house, whose cellar had been turned into a machine-gun nest.

With a roar the building collapsed, a bright flicker of flames springing out of the ruins. As though it were a signal every machine-gun, every rifle in the village opened fire on the impassive shapes at the crest of the hill. The uproar was terrific.

The shining monsters paid no more attention to it than to the rain. One of them slid gently forward a few yards, turned its trunk toward the spouting trenches and in short bursts loosed five quick bolts. There were as many spurts of flame, a few puffs of earth and the trenches became silent.

Ben Ruby's voice came through. "Retreat everybody. Atlantic City if you can make it."

With a great round fear gripping his heart Murray Lee threw in the clutch of his machine and headed in the direction he remembered as that of the main road through the town toward Atlantic City. The night had become inky-black.

Only by an occasional match or flashlight glare could the way be seen but such light as there was showed the road already filled with fugitives.

But through the rout there plowed a little company of infantry, revealed in a shellburst, keeping tight ranks as though at drill, officers at the head, not flying but retreating from a lost battle with confidence, ready to fight again the next day.

The dancing beam of a searchlight picked them out for a moment. Murray looked at them and the fear died within him. He slowed up his machine, ran it off the road and out to the left, where there seemed to be a clearing that opened in the direction of the town. After all, he could at least observe the progress of the monsters and report on them.

He was astonished to find that he had come nearly a mile from the center of the disturbance. Down there the glittering monsters, still brightly illumined by searchlight and flare, seemed to be standing still amid the outer houses of the town.

From time to time one of the things, perhaps annoyed at the pointlessness of what it saw, would swing its trunk around and discharge a light-bolt at house, barn or other object. The object promptly caved in and, if it were wood, began to burn.

Now that he could see them clearly Murray noted that they were all of fifty or sixty feet long. Their polished sides seemed one huge mirror, bright as glass, and a phosphorescent glow hung about their tails. Along either side was a slender projection like the bilge-keel of a ship, terminating about three quarters of the way along, with a small dot of the phosphorescence at its tip. They seemed machines rather than animate objects.

He was recalled to duty by the flash of light at his control board and a voice from the radiophone ". . . to all units," came the message. "Railroad Battery Fourteen about to fire on enemy tanks in Waterford. Request observation for corrections. . . . General Stanhope to all units. Railroad Battery Fourteen, twelve-inch guns, about to fire on enemy tanks in Waterford. Request observation for correction. . . ."

"Lieutenant Lee, American Tank Corps, to General Stanhope," he called into the phone. "Go ahead with Railroad Battery Fourteen. Am observing fire from east of town."

Even before he had finished speaking there was a dull rumble in the air and a tremendous heave of earth behind and to one side of the shining enemy not two hundred yards away.

"Lieutenant Lee to Railroad Battery Fourteen," he called delightedly. "Two hundred yards over, ten yards right."

Berroum! Another of the twelve-inch shells fell somewhere ahead of the giants in the village.

As Murray shouted the correction one of the metal creatures lifted its snout toward the source of the explosion curiously and, as if it had not quite understood its meaning, fired a light-beam at it. Another shell fell, just to one side.

"Lieutenant Lee, American Tank Corps, to Railroad Battery Fourteen—suggest you use armor-piercing shell. Enemy tanks appear to be armored," he called and had the comforting reply.

"Check, Lieutenant Lee. We are using armor-piercers."

Slam! Another of the twelve-inch shells struck, not ten yards behind the enemy. The ground around them rocked. One of them turned as though to examine the burst, the other lifted its snout skyward and released a long, thin beam of blue light, not in the least like the light-ray. It did not seem to occur to either of them that these shells might be dangerous. They seemed merely interested.

And then—the breathless watchers in the thickets around the doomed town saw a huge red explosion, a great flower of flame that leaped to the heavens, covered with a cloud of thick smoke, pink in the light of the burning houses.

As it cleared away there lay one of the monsters on its side, gaping and rent, the mirrored surface scarred, the phosphorescent glow extinguished, the prehensile snout drooping lifelessly. Murray Lee was conscious of dancing out of his tank and joining someone else in an embrace of delight. They were not invincible then.

"Hooray!" he cried. *"Hooray!"*

"That and twelve times over," said his companion.

That phrase struck him as familiar. For the first time he looked at his fellow celebrant. It was Gloria.

"Why, where in the world did you come from?"

"Where did you? I've been here all the time, ever since Ben ordered us home. Didn't think I'd run out on all the fun, did you? Are those things alive?"

"How do I know? They look it but you never can tell with all the junk that comet left around the earth. They might be just some new kind of tank full of dodos."

"Yeh, but . . ." The buzzing roar of one of the light-rays crashing into a clump of trees not a hundred yards away recalled them to themselves. Gloria looked up, startled. The other monster was moving slowly forward, systematically searching the hillside with its weapon.

"Say, son," she said, "I think it's time to go away from here."

But the conference at Headquarters in Hammonton that night was anything but cheerful. "It comes to this then," said General Grierson, the commander-in-chief of the expedition. "We have nothing that is effective against these dodo tanks but the twelve-inch railroad artillery, using armor-piercing shell and securing a direct hit.

"Our infantry is worse than useless. The tanks are useless. The artillery cannot get through the armor of these things although it damages the enemy artillery in the back areas."

Ben Ruby rubbed a metal chin. "Well, that isn't quite all, sir. One of the American tanks was hit and came through—damaged, I'll admit. The lightning or light-ray these dodos threw, penetrated the outer skin but not the inner. We could build more tanks of this type."

General Grierson drummed on the table. "And arm them with what? You couldn't mount a twelve-inch gun in a tank if you wanted to and we haven't any twelve-inch guns to spare."

One of the staff men looked up. "Has air bombing been tried on these—things. It seems to me that a one or two-thousand-pound bomb would be as effective as a twelve-inch shell."

"That was tried this afternoon," said the head of the air service. "The one hundred and thirty-eighth bombing squadron attacked a group of these tanks. Unfortunately the tanks kept within range of their light-ray artillery and the entire squadron was shot down."

"Mmm," said the staff man. "Let's add up the information we have secured so far and see where it leads. First they have a gun which shoots a ray that is effective either all along its length or when put up in packages like a shell and is rather like a bolt of lightning in its effect. Any deductions from that?"

"Might be electrical," said someone.

"Also might not," countered Walter Beeville. "Remember the *Melbourne's* turret. No electrical discharge would produce chemical changes like that in Krupp steel."

"Second," said the officer, "they appear to have three main types of fighting machines or individuals. First there are the dodos themselves. We know all about them and our planes can beat them—good.

"Second is their artillery—a large type that throws a beam of this emanation and a smaller type which throws it in the form of shells. Third, are these—tanks, which may themselves be the individuals we are fighting.

"They are capable of projecting these discharges for a short distance—something over four thousand yards—and apparently do not have the power of projecting it in a prolonged beam like their artillery. They are about fifty feet long, fish shaped, heavily armored and have some unknown method of propulsion. Check me if I'm wrong."

"The projection of these lightning-rays would seem to indicate they are machines," offered General Grierson hopefully.

"Not on your life," said Beeville. "Think of the electric eel."

"As I was saying," said the staff man, "our chief defect seems to be a lack of information and . . ."

General Grierson brought his fist down on the table. "Gentlemen! This discussion is leading us nowhere. We are facing one of the greatest dangers the earth has ever experienced and must take immediate measures.

"Unless someone has something more fruitful than this conference has provided thus far I shall be forced to order the reembarkation of the army and sail for home. My duty is to the citizens of the federated governments and I cannot uselessly sacrifice more lives. Our supply of railroad artillery is utterly inadequate to withstand the numbers of our adversaries. Has anyone anything to offer?"

There was a silence around the conference table, but at the moment there came a tap at the door. "Come," called General Grierson. An apologetic under-officer entered. "I beg your pardon, sir, but one of the iron Americans is here and insists that he has something of vital importance to the General. He will not go away without seeing you."

"All right. Bring him in."

There stepped into the room another of the mechanical Americans, a man neither Ben Ruby nor Beeville had ever seen before. A stiff wire brush of moustache stood out over his mouth. He wore no clothes but a kind of loin-cloth made apparently of a sheet. The metal plates of his powerful body glittered in the lamplight as he stepped forward. "General Grierson?"

"I am General Grierson."

"I'm Lieutenant Herbert Sherman of the U.S. Army Air Force. I have just escaped from the Lassans and came to offer you my services. I imagine your technical men might wish to know how they operate their machines and what would be effective against them and I think I can tell you."

Eleven

Herbert Sherman had wakened with a vague sense of something wrong and lay back in his seat for a moment, trying to remember. Everything seemed going quietly, the machine running with subdued efficiency. It came to him with a jerk—he could not hear the motor.

With the subconscious concentration of the flying man on

his ship he glanced at the instrument board first and, taking in the astonishing information that both the altimeter and the air-speed meter registered zero, he looked over the side. His vision met the familiar dentilated line of the buildings surrounding the Jackson Heights airport with a tree plastered greenly against one of them. Queer.

Then another oddity struck his attention. He recalled very clearly that he had been flying over the white landscape of winter—but now there was a tree in full leaf. Something was wrong.

As he swung himself over the side his eye caught the glint of an unfamiliar highlight on the back of his hand and with the same stupefaction that Murray Lee was contemplating the same phenomenon several miles away he perceived that, instead of a flesh-and-blood member, he had somehow acquired an iron hand. The other was the same—and the arm—and the section of stomach which presently appeared when he tore loose his shirt to look at it.

Muttering to himself he trudged across the flying field, noting that it was grown up with daisies and far from newly rolled, to the hangars. He pounded at the door, then tried it. It was unlocked. Inside someone sat tilted back in a chair against the wall, a cap pulled over his face. Sherman walked over to the sleeper, favoring him with a vigorous shake. "Hey!"

To his surprise the stranger tilted sharply over to one side and went to the floor with a bang, remaining in the position he had assumed. Sherman bent over, tugging at the cap. The man was metallic as himself but with a difference—he was solid statue cast in what seemed to be bronze.

"For Heaven's sake!" said Herbert Sherman to himself.

There seemed to be nothing in particular he could do about it. However, the sun was high and the town lay outside the door.

He spent a good deal of the day wandering about Jackson Heights, contemplating such specimens of humanity as remained in the streets, fixed in the various ungraceful and unattractive attitudes of life. He had always been a solitary and philosophical soul and he felt neither loneliness nor overwhelming curiosity as to the nature of the catastrophe which had stopped the wheels of civilization.

Toward evening, he returned to the flying field and examined his machine. One wing showed the effect of weathering but it was all-metal, of the latest model and had withstood the ordeal well. The gasoline gauge showed an empty tank but it was no great task to get more from the big underground tanks at the field. Oil lines and radiators seemed all tight.

With a kind of secret satisfaction gurgling within him Herbert Sherman taxied across the field, put the machine into a climb and went forth to have a look at New York.

He thought he could see smoke over central Manhattan and swung in that direction. The disturbance seemed to be located at the old Metropolitan Opera House which, as he approached it, seemed to have been burning but had now sunk to a pile of glowing embers. The fire argued human presence of some kind. He took more height and looked down. Times Square held a good many diminutive dots but they didn't seem to be moving.

He swung over to examine the downtown district. All quiet. When he returned he saw a car dodging across Forty-second Street and realizing that he could find human companionship whenever he needed it, which he did not at present, he returned to the flying field.

At this point it occurred to him to be hungry. Reasoning the matter out in the light of his mechanical experience he drank a pint or more of lubricating oil and searched for a place to spend the night.

Not being sleepy he raided a drug store where books were sold, took as much of its stock as he could use. Arranging one of the flares at the field in a position convenient for reading he settled down for the night. In the course of it he twice tried smoking and found that his new makeup had ruined his taste for tobacco.

With the first streaks of day he was preparing for a long flight. He had no definite purpose in mind beyond a look around the country. Was it all like this or only New York?

As he flew along toward the Newark airport a shadow fell athwart the wing and he looked up.

A big bird was soaring past, flying above and fully as fast as the plane. In his quick glance Sherman caught something unfamiliar about its flight and leaned over to snap on the mechanical pilot while he had another look.

The bird, if bird it was, was certainly a queer specimen. It seemed to have two sets of wings and was using them as though it were an airplane, the fore pair outstretched and rigid, the hind wings vibrating rapidly. As he gazed at the bird it drew ahead of the plane, gave a few quick flips to its fore-wings and banked around to pick him up again.

It was coming closer and regarding him with an uncommonly intelligent and by no means friendly eye. Sherman swung his arm at it and gave a shout—to which the bird paid not the slightest attention. Newark was running away under him.

Reluctantly, he made for the airport. It occurred to him that this would be an awkward customer if it chose to attack him and he meditated on the possibility of finding a gun in Newark.

The field was bumpy but he taxied to a stop and climbed out to look over the silent hangars before one of which a little sports plane stood dejectedly, a piece of torn wing flapping in the breeze. He looked back at the bird. It was soaring away up in a close spiral, emitting a series of screams. Sherman determined to find a gun without delay.

Newark was like Jackson Heights—same stony immobility of

inhabitants, same sense of life stopped at full tide in the streets. He prowled around till he found a hardware store and possessed himself of a fine .50-50 express rifle with an adequate supply of cartridges as well as a revolver, added to it a collection of small tools, stopped in at a library to get a supply of reading matter more to his taste than that the drug store could provide.

As he took off again, two specks in the sky far to the north represented, he decided, additional specimens of the peculiar bird life that had spread abroad since the change. How long it had been he had no idea.

Port Jervis was his first control point but Sherman was fond enough of the green wooded slopes of the Catskills to run a little north of his course, bumpy though the air was over the mountains. He set the automatic pilot and leaned back in his seat to enjoy the view.

Just north of Central Valley something seemed different about the hillside. A new scar had appeared along its edge. He turned to examine it, swooping as he did so and saw that the great forest trees, maples and oaks, were all down, twisted, barren, leafless, along a line that ran right up the valley and across the hill as though they had been harrowed by some gigantic storm. The line was singularly definite. There were no half-broken trees.

He swooped for another look and at that moment was conscious of the beat of swift wings and above the roar of the motor heard the scream of one of the strange four-winged birds.

Half-unconsciously he went into a steep climb, just as the bird flew past him on whistling pinions, and recovered to rise again in pursuit. Sherman flattened out, snapped in the automatic pilot and reached for his gun.

As he bent there came a sharp crack from above and behind him and another scream right overhead. He looked over his shoulder to see a second bird clutching at the edge of the cockpit with one giant claw. its forewings fluttering rapidly in the effort to keep its balance in the propeller's slipstream. With the other claw it grabbed and grabbed for him.

Sherman flattened himself and fired up and back, once—twice—three times. The plane rocked. The bird let go with a shrill scream, a spurt of blood showing on its chest feathers and as Sherman straightened up he saw it whirling down, wings beating wildly, uselessly, the red spot spreading.

But he had no time for more than a glance. The other bird was whirling up to the attack beneath him, yelling as though it were shouting a battle-cry. The pistol, half-empty, might too easily miss.

Sherman sought the rifle and at that moment felt the impact of a swift blow on the floor of the plane. The bird understood that he had weapons and was attacking him from beneath to avoid them! He leaned over the side, trying to get a shot at his enemy.

Beneath the plane he caught a momentatiry glimpse of the ground again, torn and tortured, and in the center of the devastation the ruins of a farmhouse, its roof canting crazily over a pulled-out wall.

The bird dodged back and forth, picking now and then at the bottom of the plane with its armored beak. He leaned further trying to get in a shot and drew a chorus of yells from the bird but no more definite result.

Suddenly from below and behind him there rose a deep humming roar, low pitched and musical. Abruptly the screaming of the bird ceased. It dropped suddenly away, its forewings folded, the rear wings spread glider-like as it floated to the ground.

He turned to look in the direction of the sound and as he turned a great glare of light sprang forth from somewhere behind, striking him full in the eyes with blinding force. At the same moment something pushed the plane forward and down.

He could feel the plane give beneath him. As he fell a wave of burning heat struck his back and the sound of a mighty torrent reached his ears. There was a crash and everything went out in a confusion of light, heat and sound.

When he recovered consciousness the first thing he saw was a blue dome, stretched so far above his head that it might have been the sky save for the fact that the light it gave had neither glare nor shadow. He puzzled idly over this for a moment, then tried to turn his head. It would not move.

"That's queer," thought Herbert Sherman and attempted to lift an arm. The hands responded readily enough but the arms were immovable. With an effort he tried to lift his body and discovered that he was held tightly by some force he could not feel.

Herbert Sherman was a patient man but not a meek one. He opened his mouth and yelled—a good loud yell with a hard swearword at the end of it. Then he stood still for a moment, listening. There was a sound that might be interpreted as the patter of feet somewhere but no one came near him. So he yelled again, louder if possible.

This time results accrued with a rapidity that was almost startling. A vivid bluish light struck him in the face, making him blink, then was turned off and he heard a clash of gears and a hum that might be that of a motor.

A moment later he felt himself lifted, whirled around, dropped with a plunk and the blue dome overhead began to flow past at rapidly mounting speed to be blotted out in a grey dimness. He perceived he was being carried down some kind of a passage whose ceiling consisted of dark stone. A motor whirred rapidly.

The stone ceiling vanished; another blue dome, less lofty, took its place. The object on which he was being carried stopped with a mechanical click and he was lifted, whirled around again and deposited on some surface. Out of the corner of his eye he caught a glimpse of something round, of a shining black coloring, with pinkish highlights, like the head of some enormous beast. He wiggled his fingers in angry and futile effort.

He was flopped over on his face and found himself looking straight down at a gray mass which from its feel on nose and chin, appeared to be rubber.

He yelled again with rage and vexation and in reply received a tap over the head with what felt like a rubber hose. He felt extraordinarily helpless. And as the realization came that he *was* helpless, without any control of what was going on, he relaxed. Some kind of examination was in progress. There was the sound of soft-treading feet behind him.

After a slight pause he was bathed in a red light of such intensity as to press upon him with physical solidity. He closed his eyes and as he did so felt a terrible pain in the region of his spine.

He gripped metallic teeth together firmly in an effort to fight the pain, and heard a clatter of metal instruments. Then the pain ceased, the light went off and something was clamped about his head.

A minute more and he had been flipped over on his back. With the same whirring of motors that had attended his arrival he was carried back through the passage and into the hall of the blue dome. He was still held firmly but now he could wiggle in his bonds.

With a clicking of machinery he was tilted up on the plane that held him. A hole yawned before his feet and he slid rapidly down a smooth incline, through a belt of darkness to drop in a heap on something soft. The trapdoor clicked with finality behind him.

He found himself, unbound, on a floor of rubber-like texture and perceived that he was in a cell with no visible exit, whose walls were formed by a heavy criss-cross grating of some red metal.

It was a little more than ten feet square. In the center a seat with curving outlines rose from the floor, apparently made of the same rubbery material as the floor itself.

A metallic track ended just in front of the seat.

Following back his eyes caught the outlines of a kind of lectern, now pushed against a wall of the cell, with spaces below the reading flat and handles attached. Against the back wall of the cell stood a similar device, but larger and without any metal track. Beside it two handles dangled from the wall on cords of flexible wire.

This was all his brief glance told him about the confines of his new home. Looking beyond it he saw that he was in one of a row of similar cells, stretching back in both directions. In front of the row of cells was a corridor along which ran a brightly-burnished metal track and this was lined by another row of cells on the farther side.

The cell at Sherman's right was empty but he observed that the one on the left had a tenant—a metal man, like himself and yet—somehow unlike. He stepped over to the grating that separated them. "What is this place, anyway?" he inquired.

His neighbor, who had been sitting in the rubber chair, turned toward him a round and foolish face with a long naked upper lip and burst into a flood of conversation of which Sherman could not understand one word.

He held up his hand. "Wait a minute. Go slow. I don't get you."

The expression on the fellow's face changed to one of wonderment. He made another effort at conversation, accompanying it with gestures. "Wait," said Sherman. *"Sprechen Sie Deutsch? Francais? Habla Espanol?* No? I don't know any Italian."

No use. The metal face remained blankly uninspired. Sherman went through the motions of drawing from his pocket a phantom cigarette, applying to it an imaginary match and blowing the smoke in the air.

It is impossible for a man whose forehead is composed of a series of lateral metal bands to frown. If it were the other would have done so. Then he stepped across to his lectern and *with his toes* pulled the bottom slide open, extracted from it a round rubber container and, reaching through the bars, handed it to Sherman.

The airman understood the difference that had puzzled him in the beginning. Instead of the graceful backsweeping curve that sets a man's head vertical with his body, this individual had the round-curve neck and low-hung head of the ape.

Twelve

To hide his surprise Sherman bent his head to examine the object the ape-man had handed him. It was about the size of a baseball with little holes in it. He inserted a finger in one of the holes and a stream of oil squirted out and struck him in the eye.

His neighbor gave a cry of annoyance at his clumsiness and reached through the bars to have the ball returned. As he received it there came sudden flickerings of lights along the hall from somewhere high up, like the trails of blue and green rockets. The mechanical ape-man dropped the oil-ball and dashed to the front of his cell.

Sherman saw a vehicle proceeding down the line of cells—a kind of truck that rode on the track of the corridor and was so wide it just missed the gratings. It had a long series of doors in its sides and as it came opposite an occupied cell it stopped. Something happened. The bars of the cell opened inward and the inmate emerged to step into a compartment which at once closed behind him.

When it stopped at the ape-man's cage Sherman watched the procedure closely. A little arm appeared from beneath the door of the compartment and did something to one of the lower bars of the cell. But the truck passed Sherman by, moving silently along to other cells beyond him.

He turned to examine the room more closely and as he did so saw that a second truck was following the first. This one, with an exactly reversed procedure, was returning robots to their cells. It dropped an inmate in the cell at his right—(another ape-man)—and trundled along down the line. But as it reached the end of the corridor it turned back and, running along till it came to his cell, stopped, flung out the metal arm and opened the bars in invitation.

Sherman had no thought of disobeying. As long as he was in this queerest of all possible worlds, he thought, he might as well keep to the rules. But he was curious about the joint of the cage and how it unlocked and he paused a moment to examine it.

The machine before him buzzed impatiently. He lingered. There came a sudden clang of metal from inside the car, a vivid beam of blue light called his attention, and looking up, he saw the word EXIT printed in letters of fire at the top of the compartment.

With a smile he stepped in. A soft light was turned on and he found himself in a tiny cubbyhole with just room for the single seat it provided and on which he seated himself. There was no window.

The machine carried him along smoothly for perhaps five minutes, stopped and the door opened before him. He issued into another blue-domed hall—a small one this time, containing a rubber seat like that in his cell but with an extended arm on which rested a complex apparatus of some kind. The seat faced a white screen like those in movie theaters.

He seated himself and at once a series of words appeared in dark green on the screen. *Dominance was not complete,* it read. *Communication?* Then below, in smaller type, as though it were the body of a newspaper column. *Lassans service man. Flier writing information through communication excellent. Dinner, bed, book. No smoking. Yours very truly.*

As he gazed in astonishment at this cryptic collection of words it was erased and its place was taken by a picture which he recognized as a likeness of himself in his present metallic state. A talking picture, which made a few remarks in the same incomprehensible gibberish the ape-man had used, then sat down in a chair like that in which he now rested and proceeded to write on the widespread arm with a stylus which was attached to it. The screen went blank. Evidently he was supposed to communicate something by writing.

The stylus was a metal pencil and the material of the arm, though not apparently metallic, must be, he argued from the fact that it seemed to have electric connections attached. As he examined it, the blue light flickered at him impatiently. *The white knight*, he wrote in a fit of impish perversity, *is climbing up the poker*. Instantly the words flashed on the screen.

Pause. IS CLIMBING declared the screen, in capitals. Then below it appeared a fairly creditable picture of a knight in armor followed by a not very creditable picture of a poker. Sherman began to comprehend. Whoever it was behind this business had managed a correspondence course of a sort in English but had failed to learn the verbs and he was being asked to explain.

For answer he produced a crude drawing of a monkey climbing a stick and demonstrated the action by getting up and going through the motions of climbing. Immediately the screen flashed a picture of the knight in armor ascending the poker by the same means.

But it had hardly appeared before it was wiped out to be replaced by a flickering of blue lights and an angry buzz. His interlocutor had seen the absurdity of the sentence and was demanding a more serious approach to the problem. For answer Sherman wrote, *Where am I and who are you?*

A longer pause. *Dominance not complete*, said the screen. Then came the picture of the first page of a child's ABC book with A *was an Archer who shot at a frog*, below the usual childish picture. Then came the word *think*. With the best will in the world Sherman was puzzled to illustrate this idea but by tapping his forehead and drawing a crude diagram of the brain as he remembered it from books, he managed to give some satisfaction.

The process went on for three or four hours as nearly as Sherman could judge the time, ending with a flash of the word *Exit* in red from the screen and a dimming of the blue-dome light. He turned toward the door and found the car that had brought him.

As it rumbled back to his cell he ruminated on the fact that none of the men, or whatever they were behind this place had yet made themselves visible.

But what next? He pondered the question as the car deposited him in his cell. Obviously he was being kept a prisoner.

The first thing that suggested itself was a closer inspection of his cell. The lectern yielded an oil-ball like that the ape-man had given him and another similar device containing grease. There were various tools and in the last drawer he examined a complete duplicate set of wrist and finger joints.

The larger cupboard had deep drawers, mostly empty, though one of them contained a number of books—*Mystery of Old-*

mixon Hall, Report of the Smithsonian Institution, 1903, The Poems of Jerusha G. White—a depressing collection.

This seemed to exhaust the possibilities of the cell and Sherman looked about for further amusement. His ape neighbor had pressed himself close to the bars on that side, indicating his interest in what Sherman was doing by chuckling.

Further down the line one of the ape-men was holding the pair of handles that projected from the wall beside his cabinet. Sherman grasped his also. There was a pleasant little electric shock and in the center of the wall before him a slide moved back to disclose a circle of melting light that changed color and form in pleasing variations.

The sensation was enormously invigorating and it struck the man with surprise that this must be the way these creatures— "These creatures!" he thought, "I'm one of them"—the way these creatures acquired nourishment.

"Hey!" he called in a voice loud enough to carry throughout the room. "Is there anyone here that can understand what I'm saying?"

There was a clank of metal as faces turned in his direction all down the line of cages. "Yes, I guess so," called a voice from about thirty feet away.

Sherman felt an overwhelming sense of relief. "Who's got us here and why are they keeping us here?" he shouted back.

A moment's silence. Then—"Near's I can make out it's a passel of elephants and they've got us here to work."

"What?"

"Work! Make you punch the holes on these light machines. It wears your fingers off and you have to screw new ones in at night."

"No, I mean about the elephants."

"That's what I said—elephants. They wear pants and they're right smart too."

"Who are you?"

"Mellen, Harve Mellen. I had a farm right here where they set up this opry house of theirs."

Along the edge of Sherman's cell a blue light began to blink. He had an uncomfortable sensation of being watched. "Is there any way of getting out of here?"

"Sssh," answered the other. "Them blue lights mean you to shut up. You'll get a paste in the eye with the yaller lights if you don't."

So that was it! They were being held as the servants—slaves —of some unseen and powerful and very, very watchful intelligence.

It must be an actual invasion of the earth, as in H. G. Wells' *War of the Worlds*, a book he had read in his youth. The comet could have been no comet then and . . .

They were giving him books, food—if this electrical thing

was indeed the food his new body required—little to do. Keeping him a prisoner in a kind of poisoned paradise.

At all events the locks on these bars should offer no great difficulty to a competent mechanic. He set himself to a further examination of the tools in the lectern.

The main difficulty in the way of any plan of escape lay in his complete lack of both information and the means of obtaining it.

On the second day, out of curiosity, Sherman kept up the conversation after the blue lights went on. A vivid stream of yellow light promptly issued from the corner of the cage, striking him full in the eyes. Apparently it was accompanied by some kind of a force-ray for he found himself stretched flat on the floor. After that he did not repeat the experiment.

The next question was that of the lock on the cell-bars. The closest inspection he could give did not reveal the joints—they were extraordinarily well fitted. On the other hand he remembered that the arm of the truck had reached under one of the lower bars. Lying flat on his back Sherman pulled himself along from bar to bar, inspecting each in turn.

About midway along the front of the cell, he perceived a tiny orifice in the base of one bar—a mere pinhole. Marveling at the delicacy of the adjustment which could use so tiny a hole as a lock he sat down to consider the problem. He was completely naked and had nothing but the objects that had been placed in the cell by his jailers.

Among the assortment of tools in his bureau was a curve-bladed knife with the handle set parallel to the blade as though it were meant for chopping. Forming the wall of the same drawer was a strip of a material like emery cloth. After some experimenting he found a fingerhole which, when squeezed, caused this emery-cloth to revolve, giving a satisfactory abrasive.

Thus armed with a tool and a means of keeping an edge on it, he took one of the metal bands from the drawer that contained the duplicate set of hands and set to work.

Producing a needle that would penetrate the hole in the bars took all of three days' work though he had no means of marking the time accurately. The metal band was pliable, light and, for all its pliability and lightness, incredibly hard. His tool would barely scratch it and required constant sharpenings. Moreover, he had little time to himself; his unseen scholar required constant lessons in English. But at last the task was done.

Choosing a moment when one of the cages at his side was empty and the occupant of the other was busy tossing a ball from one hand to another, Sherman lay down on the floor, found the opening and drove his needle home. Nothing happened.

He surveyed the result with disappointment. But it occurred to him that perhaps he had not learned the whole secret of the arm, and the next time the car came down the corridor for him he was lying on the floor, carefully watching the opening.

As he had originally surmised a needle-point was driven home. But he noted that on either side of the point the arm gripped the bar tightly, pressing it upward.

This presented another difficulty. He had only two hands. If one of them worked the needle he could grip the bar in only one place. But he remembered, fortunately, that his toes now had a remarkable power of prehension.

He finally succeeded in bracing himself in a curiously twisted attitude and driving the needle home under the proper auspices. To his delight it worked—when the needle went in the bars opened in the proper place, swinging back into position automatically as the pressure was withdrawn.

With a new sense of freedom Sherman turned to the next step. This was to find out more of the place in which he was confined.

But even on this point he was not to be long without enlightenment. His unseen pupil in English was making most amazing progress. The white screen which was their means of communication now bore complicated messages about such subjects as what constituted philosophy.

Sherman felt himself in contact with an exceptionally keen and active mind, though one to which the simplest earthly ideas were unfamiliar. There were queer misapprehensions—for instance, he couldn't seem to make the unseen scholar understand the use and value of money and they labored for a whole day over *president* and *political*.

In technical matters it was otherwise. Sherman had barely to express an idea before the screen made it evident that the auditor had grasped its whole purport. When he wrote the word *atom* for instance and tried to give a faint picture of the current theory of the atom it was hardly a second before the screen flashed up with a series of diagrams and mathematical formulae, picturing and explaining atoms of different types.

After four weeks or more, the car that came for him one day discharged him into a room entirely different from the schoolroom. It was small and some twenty feet across. Against the wall opposite the door stood a huge machine, the connections of which seemed to go back through the wall. Its vast complex of pulleys, valves and rods conveyed no hint of its purpose even to his mechanically-trained mind.

Across the front of it was a long blackboard, four feet or more across and somewhat like the instrument board of an airplane in general character. At the top of this board was a band of ground glass set off in divisions. Beneath this band a series of holes, each just large enough to admit a finger, each marked off by a character of some kind in no language Sherman had ever seen.

To complete the picture one of the mechanical ape-men stood

before the board as though expecting him. On the ape-man's head was a tight-fitting helmet, connecting with some part of the machine by a flexible tube. As Sherman entered the room the ape-man motioned him over to the board, pointed to the holes and said, "Watch!"

A flash of purple light appeared behind the first of the ground-glass screens. The ape-man promptly thrust his finger into the first of the holes. The light went out, and the ape-man turned to Sherman. "Do," he said. The light flashed on again and Sherman did as his instructor had done.

He was rewarded by a tearing pain in the fingertip and withdrew the member at once. Right at the end it had become slightly gray. The ape-man smiled. Behind the second ground-glass a red light now appeared and the ape-man thrust his finger into another of the apertures, indicating that Sherman should imitate him.

This time, Sherman was more cautious but as he delayed the light winked angrily. Again he received the jerk of pain in the fingertip and withdrew it to find that the gray spot had spread.

When the third light flashed on he refused to copy the motion of his instructor. The light blinked at him insistently. He placed both hands behind his back and stepped away from the machine. The apeman threw back his head and emitted a long, piercing howl.

Almost immediately the door slid back and the car appeared. As Sherman stepped to its threshold, it thrust forth a gigantic folding claw which gripped him firmly around the waist and held him while a shaft of the painful yellow light was thrown into his eyes—then tossed him back on the floor.

Dazed by the light and the fall Herbert Sherman rolled on the floor, thoughts of retaliation flashing through his head. But he was no fool, and before he had even picked himself up, he realized that his present case was hopeless. Gritting his teeth he set himself to follow the ape-man's instructions.

The course of instruction was not particularly difficult to memorize. It seemed that for each color of light behind the ground-glass panels one must thrust a finger into a different one of the holes below—hold it there in spite of the pain till the colored light went out—then remove it.

After an hour or two of it, when he had learned to perform the various operations with mechanical precision and the tip of his index finger had already begun to scale off, the ape-man smiled at him, waved approval and reaching down beneath the blackboard, pulled out a drawer from which he extracted a fingertip, made of the same metal as those he already bore, and proceeded to show Sherman how to attach it.

As a mechanic he watched the process with some interest. The "bone" of the finger, with its joint, screwed cunningly into the bone of the next joint below, the lower end of the screw be-

ing curiously cut away and having a tiny point of wire set in it.
The muscular bands had loose ends that merely tucked in but
so well were they fashioned, that once in position, it was impossible to pull them out until the fingertip had been unscrewed.

The instruction process over, he was returned to his cell,
wondering what was to happen next.

Thirteen

When the car next called for him it took a much longer course
—a twenty-minute ride—and when he stepped out it was not
into a room of any kind but in what appeared to be a tunnel
cut in the living rock, at least six feet wide and fully twice as
high. The rock on all sides had been beautifully smoothed by
some unknown hand, except underfoot, where it had been left
rough enough to give a grip to the feet.

At his side were two of the ape-men, who had been released
from the car at the same time. The tunnel led them straight
ahead for a distance, then dipped and turned to the right. As
he rounded the corner he could see that it ended below and before him in a room where machinery whirred.

The ape-men went straight on, looking neither to the right
nor the left. As they reached the door that gave into the machine-room they encountered another ape-man, wearing the
same kind of helmet with its attached tube that Sherman's instructor had worn.

The ape-men who came with him stopped. The helmeted one
looked at them stupidly for a moment and then, as though obey-
ing some unspoken command, took him by the arm and led him
across the room to the front of a machine and there thrust one
of the ubiquitous helmets on his head.

The machine, as nearly as Sherman could make out, was a
duplicate of that on which he had injured his fingers. As the helmet was buckled on the apeman who stood before it he immediately began to watch the ground-glass panels and put his fingers
in the holes below.

The process was repeated with the second apeman, and then
the sentinel returned to Sherman. Taking him by the arm the
mechanical beast led him past the row of machines—there
seemed to be only four in the room—and to a door at one
side, giving him a gentle push. It was the opening of another
tunnel, down which Sherman walked for some forty or fifty
yards before encountering a second door and a second helmeted
ape-man sentry.

This one took him by the arm and led him across the room to
a machine, where it left him. Sherman perceived that he was
supposed to care for it and with a sigh bent to his task.

It was some moments before the rapid flashing of lights gave him a respite. Then he had an opportunity to look about him and observed that, as in the other room, there were four machines. Two of them were untenanted but at the one next to his there was someone working. When he glanced again he was sure it was a mechanized human like himself—and a girl!

"What is this place?" he asked, "and who are you?"

The other gave a covert glance over his shoulder at the sentry by the door. "Sssh!" she said out of the corner of her mouth. "Not so loud. I'm Marta Lami—and I think this place is hell!"

After a time they contrived a sort of conversation, a word at a time, with covert glances at the ape-man sentry.

"Who is keeping us here?" asked Sherman.

"Don't know," she replied. "Think it's the elephants."

"What elephants?" he asked a word at a time. "I haven't seen any."

"You will. They come around and inspect what you're doing. Are you new here?"

"New at these machines. They had me teaching them to write English. This is my first day in here."

"This is my eightieth work-period. We lost track of the days."

"So did I. Where are we? Are there any other humans with you?"

"One in the cage across the corridor from me. Walter Stevens, the Wall Street man."

"Have they got him on this job, too?"

"Yes."

"Do you know what these machines are for?"

"Stevens said they were for digging something. They had the helmets on him twice."

"What helmets?"

"Like dopey at the door wears. The dopeys all have to wear them. Haven't got any brains, I guess. I had one on once when they were teaching me to do this. They tell you what to think."

"What do you mean?"

"You put the helmet on and it's like you're hypnotized. You can't think anything but what they want you to think."

Sherman shuddered slightly.

"How did they get you?" asked the girl.

"In an airplane. They shot me down somewhere and when I came to put me in one of those cages. How did you get here?"

"The birds. I was at West Point with Stevens and that old fool Vanderschoof. They started shooting at the birds and the birds just picked us up and flew away with us."

"Where were you after you came to? I mean after the comet."

"New York. Century Roof. I was dancing there before."

"You aren't Marta Lami, the dancer?"

"Sure. Who do you think?"

He turned and regarded her deliberately, careless of the aroused attention of the sentry. So this was the famous dancer! How little she resembled it now, a parody of the human form, working her fingers off as the slave of an alien and conquering race.

She asked the next question. "Where have they got you?"

"I don't know. In a cage somewhere. The only people around there are like those mugs."

"I wonder how long they'll keep us at this."

"I wish I could tell you. How's chances of making a break?"

"Rotten. There was a guy at the next machine tried three or four work-periods ago. He socked the dopey at the door."

"What happened?"

"They sent a machine down for him and gave him the yellow lights all over. It was rugged—you should have heard him scream."

"How far down are we anyway?"

"You got me, boy friend. *Sssh!* Watch the dopey."

Sherman glanced over his shoulder to see the apeman moving aside from the door and bent back to his work. Evidently something important was imminent.

Down the passage came something moving—something flesh-like and smooth of a pale grayblue deadfish color, like a dangling serpent, then a round bulging head, finally the full form of an elephant—but such an elephant as mortal eye had never before seen.

It stood barely eight feet high and its legs were both longer and infinitely more slender and graceful than the legs of any earthly elephant. The ears were smaller, not loose flaps of skin but possessed of definite form and pressed close to the head.

The skull was enormous, bulging at the forehead and wrinkled in the middle over the large intelligent eyes in an expression permanently cross and dissatisfied. As for the trunk it reached nearly to the floor, longer and thinner in proportion than the trunk of an ordinary elephant, at its tip divided into four fingerlike projections set around the circle of the nostril.

Oddest of all the elephant wore clothes—or at least an outer garment, a kind of long cloak which appeared to be attached underneath its body and which covered every portion from neck to ankles. The feet also were covered. A kind of parka hung back from the head on that portion of the cloak which rested on the creature's back. But what chiefly aroused Sherman's loathing was that the naked skin, wherever exposed, was of that same poisonous deadfish blue.

For a moment the thing stood in the doorway, regarding them, swinging its long trunk around restlessly as though it could tell something about them by its sense of smell. Then it advanced a step or two into the room and, placing its trunk close to Sherman's body, began to run over it, sniffing, a few inches away.

Apparently satisfied with the result of its examination the elephant turned to go, stopping as it did so to unhook some projection on the ape-man's helmet and apply it to its ear. After listening for a moment it put the end of the trunk to this projection, snorted into it and went away with soundless steps.

For several minutes the two worked on in silence after this. Then, "Well, now you've seen him. That was our boss."

"That—thing?"

"Say, those babies know more than Einstein ever heard of. Try to get fresh with one of them and see."

"What do they do?"

"Shoot you with one of the light-guns. They carry little ones with them. They melt you down wherever they hit you and you have to go to the operating room to have things put back and it hurts like blazes."

"I must have been there after they brought me down in my plane. They did something to my back."

"Then you know, chum. After that they put the helmet on you and you have to tell 'em what you're thinking about. You can beat that game, though, if you're careful. All I'd give 'em was how good a couple of Scotch highballs would taste and it made monkeys of 'em."

It was all very strange and not a little bewildering. Intelligent elephants that controlled forces beyond the powers of men—who could place a helmet on your head and read your thoughts—who could repair the new mechanized human form after it had apparently suffered irreparable damage—who treated men and women as lower animals. Their arrival must have been that of the comet.

Their plight at the hands of these master-animals was bad but it might be worse. At least he had a certain amount of freedom, he was stronger than he had ever before been in his life and felt quite as intelligent. It would be strange if he could not accomplish something.

Everything seemed to show that the operation of most of these machines was predominately electrical. It would be strange if the car that carried them to and fro was not—yes and the helmets the ape-men wore. If he could short-circuit even a part of them . . .

Apparently his new body was a good conductor and impervious to the injurious effects of the electric current. Short-circuit something, that was the idea, create confusion—and trust to escaping in the midst of it? Perhaps— Their machinery was so efficient that a child could operate it. It was in a pinch that their real intelligence would show.

It struck him that it would do little good to escape unless he

did learn something about these elephant-people, their mysterious light-guns, the vast city that they seemed to have hollowed
out of the heart of the solid Catskill rock, their chemistry and
mettallurgy and methods of attack and defense.

Otherwise escape would be a jumping from the frying-pan
into the fire.

"By the way, what do these eggs call themselves?" he asked.

"Lassans," said the dancer.

Fourteen

The first thing to be done, Sherman decided, was to short-circuit the mind-reading helmet of the guard at the door if it were
possible. He realized that he was dealing with the products of
an utterly alien form of mentality, one that might not produce
its results in the same way that an earthman would at all.

If the thing were electrical the current must come through
the tube to the top of the head. On his second work-period he
observed this tube with care. It ran through an aperture in
the stone roof and was apparently provided with some spring
device, for a considerable length of it reeled out when the ape-
man wished to walk across the room and was absorbed as he returned.

The tube seemed to be made of the rubberlike material
that composed the floor of his cage. The simplest plan, of
course, would be to bring his chopping-knife with him and,
when the ape-man paused before the wall, swing it up in a
sweep, severing the tube.

But this, he felt, would not necessarily short-circuit the current and the damage would be too readily laid at his door. The
desideratum was some damage that, apparently accidental,
would yet produce a good deal of uproar.

He talked it over with Marta Lami.

"I think you're bugs, but anything for excitement. What do
you want me to do about it?"

"Well, here's what I figured out," Sherman explained. "We
both arrive about the same time. I'll bring my knife. When we
come in you hang back a bit and while you're doing it I'll take a
poke at that cable with the knife, not enough to cut it but
enough to damage it.

"Then about halfway through the work period I'll turn
around and say something to you. If I do it quick enough I
think the monk will start for me and if the cable doesn't go
then, I'll miss my guess."

The next period proved unsuitable. The dancer's car arrived
considerably before Sherman's and the plan was dropped for

the time. But on the following occasion, as Sherman came down the passage, he noticed Marta Lami just ahead of him.

He hurried to catch up and she understood; she avoided the guard's outstretched hand and hung back a minute against the wall as Sherman came up. He made one quick motion. The cable sheared halfway through exposing two wires of bright metal.

It proved unnecessary to put the second part of the plan into operation. For just as Sherman was nerving himself to swing round and attract the apeman's attention, he heard the soft pad-pad of one of the approaching Lassans. The ape-man stepped back to clear the entrance as he had before and as he did so, there was a trickle of sparks, a blinding flash and the cable short-circuited.

The result was totally unexpected. From the great machine before Sherman there came an answering flash. The ground glass split across with a bang, there was a hissing sound and something blew up.

Sherman came to flat on his back and with pieces of rock and the debris of the machine lying across his legs. He looked around; Marta Lami lay some little distance across the room, half covered with rock, one arm flung across her eyes as though to protect them. Above the solid granite looked as though a blasting charge had been fired in its midst.

Sherman pulled himself to a sitting posture and finding nothing damaged stood upright. The machine, badly shattered, lay in fragments of bent rods, broken pulleys and wrecked cylinders all about him.

In the place where it had stood was a long narrow opening, at the bottom of which something irregular shut off a bright point of light. A blast of heat exuded from the place and a steady deep-voiced roaring was audible. The ape-man guard was nowhere to be seen.

He bent to pick up the unconscious girl, wondering how one revived a mechanical woman especially without water. She solved the problem by opening her eyes. "Who touched off the pineapple, chum?"

"I did. Come out of it and tell me what we do next. Anything busted?"

"Only my head." She patted the mass of stiff wire. "Boy, am I glad I wore my hair long before they made a robot of me!" She stood up, looked down the pit where the machine had been and said, "Say, let's get out of here. That don't look good."

"All right," said Sherman. "Which way? Wait till I get my knife."

"Leave it," she said. "Those babies are nobody's saps. If they find it on you . . . Come on, I think that thing is going to pop again."

The roaring had increased in both volume and intensity and

the machine-room had become unbearably hot. They turned toward the door but just at the entrance to the passage a pile of debris had descended, making egress impossible.

"Come on," called the dancer, tearing at the rocks. "Get these out of the road unless you want to be stewed in your own juice."

Together they toiled over the blocks of granite, hurling them backward toward the wreck of the machine. One minute, two, three—the roaring behind them grew and spread—the heat became terrific.

"*Ah!*" cried Marta Lami at last. A tiny opening at the top of the heap was before them. Sherman tugged at a rock—one more and they would be through. But it was too big.

"No, this one," shouted his companion and together they dragged at it. It gave—a cascade of smaller stones rolled down the heap to the floor.

"You first," said Sherman and stood aside.

The dancer wriggled through and reached back a hand to pull him after. He dived, grunted, pushed—made it. As they turned to slide down the other side of the heap, he looked back. A little rivulet of something white, hot and liquid was creeping through the ruins of the machine and into the room.

Up the passage, strewn with wreckage but with no more blockades, into the upper machine room. The machines here were also deserted and from one of them issued a minor variation on the roaring sound they had heard in their own room.

They turned, sped up the next passage to the place where the cars ordinarily met them. The car-track was dark. By the illumination from the passage they could see the rail on which it ran, a foot or two down from the level of the passage and about a foot broad—a single shining ribbon of metal. Sherman looked in either direction. Nothing. The roaring behind them continued.

"Drive on, chum," said Marta.

"Stop, look, listen, watch out for the cars," he quoted as they leaped down and both laughed.

The roadbed was as smooth as glass, the rail set flush with it. Judging that the best route was the one taking them upward Sherman turned to the right and they began climbing, hand in metal hand.

The track was on a curve as well as an ascent. After a few steps they were in complete darkness and could only feel their way along. They climbed for what seemed hours.

The tunnel continued dark, without branches, simply winding on and on. Finally, so quickly that Sherman missed his step, they reached a level place, rounded one more curve, saw ahead of them a band of light across the track from some side-tunnel.

"Shall we try it?"

"Might be another machineroom," she said, "but let's go.

This track is terrible. If I wasn't made of iron I'd have bruises all over."

He vaulted over the sill, reached down and hauled her after him. From behind them came the roar, sunk to a vague purring by the distance. They were in another granite-lined passage, one that went straight ahead for a few yards, then branched sharply. The right hand fork seemed to lead downward—automatically they took the other turn.

A diffused radiance from somewhere high in the walls, as though the granite had been rendered transparent here and there, filled the whole place with shadowless light. For a time the passage ran level, then it climbed again with another fork to the right, which dipped away from their level and which they again avoided. Of any other living being there was thus far no sign.

The passage began climbing again, in a tight spiral this time.

"Good thing we're in training," remarked Marta Lami. "This is worse than the stairs in the Statue of Liberty."

The spiral ended, a side passage branched off. The dancer stopped.

"*Shh*, someone's coming. Duck in here." She seized Sherman's hand and led him into the sidepassage, down which they ran for a few feet, then paused to look back.

Along the passage they had just vacated came a group of the ape-men, four or five of them, each carrying on his left arm a long, cylindrical shield like those one sees in pictures of Roman soldiers, in his right hand some instrument that looked like a fire extinguisher with a long, flexible nozzle.

Each of the group wore one of the helmets and behind them, wearing a smilar headgear to which all the tubes were connected from the ape-men's helmets came one of the Lassans. The group hurried past without a sideward glance. After a minute Sherman and the dancer crept cautiously forward. The procession had gone straight on down.

Sherman and Marta sprinted up the passage in the direction from which the ape-men and their guide had come. The passage no longer rose with the same steepness and as the ascent grew more gentle the tunnel widened, with frequent side-passages to the right and branches leading down to the track at the left.

Finally after a sharp turn it opened out into a big room, untenanted like all they had seen so far, filled with a complex maze of machinery, but machinery of a different character from that they had labored at. At the farther end of the room a door stood open. They dashed across it, plunged through—and found themselves in one of the enormous blue-domed halls, whose ceiling seemed to stretch miles above them.

It must have been all of three hundred feet across, and there was no visible support for the ceiling. All about the place stood various objects and pieces of machinery and figures moved dimly among the titanic apparatus at the far end. But what most attracted their attention was the huge object that stood right before them.

It looked like a metal fish on an enormous scale. Fully fifty feet long and twenty feet high, its proportions dwarfed everything about it. Its sides, of brilliantly polished metal, shone like a mirror. The tail came to a stubby point, from which projected a circle of four tubes.

Down the side was a rib which ended in a similar tube about halfway and at the nose-end of the mechanical fish was a ten-foot snout, not unlike an elephant's trunk in shape and apparently made of the same rubbery material which held the cables of the helmets.

Marta pulled Sherman down behind the thing and they peered around the edge, seeking a means of egress from the room. The nearest was twenty or thirty feet away. Watching their opportunity they chose a moment when they seemed least likely to attract attention and made a dive for it.

They found themselves in another passage, terminating in two doors.

"Which?" asked Sherman.

"Eeeny-meeny." said Marta. "This one." And, stepping boldly to the right hand door, pushed it open.

For a moment they could only gaze. The room they had entered was another and smaller blue-domed hall. Around its sides was a row of curious twisted benches of green material, each of which was now occupied by one of the Lassans, hood thrown back from head, elephant-trunk thrust into a large pool of some viscous green stuff with bright yellow flecks in it in the center of the circle. Half a dozen helmeted ape-men stood behind the benches of their masters, apparently serving them at this singular meal.

As the two humans entered there was one of those silences which are pregnant with events. Then, "Good evening, folks. How's things?" said Marta and curtsied gracefully.

The sound of her words seemed to release the spell. With a bellow of rage the nearest Lassan leaped from his bench, fumbling at one of the pouches in his cloak.

The light-gun! thought Sherman and braced himself to spring, but another of the masters extended his trunk and detained the first. There was a momentary babble of rumbling conversation, then one of the Lassans reached behind him, picked up a helmet and placed it on his head and, attaching a tube to one of the ape-men, rose.

The ape-man moved toward Marta and Sherman like a being in a dream. They turned to run but the Lassan produced a light-gun with such evident intention of using it at the first motion that they paused.

"Looks like we're in for it," said the dancer. "Oh, well, lead on Napoleon."

Under the direction of the Lassan the ape-man took them each by an arm and led them back through the hall of the metal fish, down among the machines, where two or three others stared at them or lifted inquisitive trunks in their direction.

Then into another passage which had been one of the inevitable cartracks. Their Lassan conductor reached around the corner into the passage, applied his trunk briefly to something and a moment later one of the cars slid silently into position. The door opened.

"So long, old pal," said Marta Lami. "Even if I never see you again we had a great time together."

"So long," replied Sherman, taking his place in the car.

The car did not take them far. It discharged Sherman in a little passage before a narrow door, which opened automatically to admit him to a small blue-domed room containing nothing but a seat, one of the benches on which he had seen the Lassans reclining and a mass of wires and tubes.

There seemed nothing in particular to do. He was at liberty save that the door closed firmly behind him, cutting off escape. Seeing that he was left alone he seated himself and began to examine the machinery, most of which was attached to his chair.

Fifteen

Before he had time to riddle out any of its secrets the door opened again and one of the Lassans came in—a distinctly different type from any he had higherto seen. This one was smaller than most. His skin, where exposed, was covered by a tracery of fine wrinkles and his coloring was whiter than the rest.

Little crowsfeet stood around the corners of his eyes, giving him an expression that was singularly humorous. He approached Sherman on noiseless feet, moved his trunk up and down as though examining him. Then, producing from a pocket in his cloak one of the thought-helmets, he set it on Sherman's head, tightened a connection or two with his trunk and, placing a like device on his own head, settled himself on the twisted bench.

The ordeal of the helmet!

To Sherman's surprise there seemed no attempt to force his mind. The thought leaped up, unbidden, *Why, this—this Lassan is friendly!* No definite image or plan or connection of ideas formed itself in his brain. He merely felt enormously soothed and strengthened.

"You are too intelligent, too high a type to have been put to work at the machines," came the thought of the Lassan. "We might better have put you at the controls of one of the fighting machines." This thought caused a mental image of the giant silver fish he had seen in the hall of the dome to rise in his mind.

"It was a mistake," the thought went on, "that you were sent here. The Alphen of the mental department, who had your case in charge, should have known better. You earthmen make much better machines than the ones we brought with us. You do not even need the helmets in order to control. Some of you are even capable of understanding and operating the lights."

This, he explained afterward, appeared not as a consecutive sentence in Sherman's mind, but as a succession of ideas, almost as though he were thinking them himself. With the word *lights* a complex picture presented itself, involving the light-guns and a large amount of other complex apparatus, whose exact uses he did not then or later understand, but which he felt he understood at the moment.

"Now," the Lassan's thought went on, "I don't blame you for being frightened and trying to run away but you know we are different and I don't quite understand what frightened you. You were working at a machine, were you not?"

And, as Sherman thought of himself sticking his fingers in the apertures of the machines, "I thought so. What happened?"

Unbidden the memory of the explosion came to him. Again he heard the Lassan's step in the corridor, saw the guard move aside, the sputter from the cable, the explosion. Then his memory jumped to the moment of tugging at the stones with the roar and heat all round and the white-hot stream in pursuit.

A vague but sympathetic thought reached him, followed by a question, "But what made that happen? You're intelligent, you understand these things, you are a mechanic—what made it happen?"

With a start of surprise Sherman realized that the Lassan had been leading him gently along from place to place—to trap him! He thought of a plate of steaming corned beef and cabbage, of the multiplication table— $5 \times 5 = 25$, all in neat rows of figures, thought of how to control a plane that had gone into a tailspin.

The pressure suddenly relaxed, the mind opposite his became friendly again. Once more he received the vague intimation of sympathy and understanding, even of admiration of his mental strength.

"Why," the thought was telling him, "you have quite as much mentality as a Lassan! That is a very high compliment. I have never before met one of the lower animals who could withhold his thoughts from me. It is most extraordinary. Is it possible for you to withhold your thoughts from your own kind as well?"

Not at all difficult, thought Sherman. Indeed the difficulty in human communication lies not in withholding thoughts but in expressing them.

His interlocutor went on, "Ah, but the feeling, the thought is generally understood though it may not be clear. Tell me, have you never withheld a thought from someone who wished to know it?"

Yes, thought Sherman, I have—and remembered a poker game at the Cleveland airport; of the time when he had thought of numerous unpleasant ways of slaying the mechanic who had left a leak in his oil-line; of the time when a girl had tried to gold-dig him and he had divined her intention first; of the time when he had lifted the knife!

Again that jar! He realized with a start that the Lassan, having failed to pick his brain with friendliness, was trying to do it with flattery. The realization so filled him with anger that he had no difficulty in resisting the pressure.

Once more the pressure relaxed. The Lassan was congratulating him again. "No, this is sincere this time and not flattery. You win. I shall not try to make you tell me again. We can probably obtain it from the other one anyway.

"Oh, man of a debased and alien race, I salute you. If your race were all like you we might breed you for intelligence and live in cooperation with you. It is almost a pity you had to be mechanized. If there is any information you wish, I will gladly exchange with you.

"We have seen your homes and we are curious—imagine living above ground—and from others of your race we know that you have many fine machines, almost a civilization in fact. We would willingly know more of it and in return will tell you of our accomplishments."

Could this offer conceal some new trap? The Lassan divined this thought as soon as formed, and reassured him. "Since we now live here and since there are so few of your folk left it is important that we know about each other. We must live side by side—why not in friendship?"

The offer seemed fair enough. At all events if there were any injudicious questions he could turn them aside and there was a good deal he wished to learn. He assented.

"Good. Suppose you ask a question and then I will. What do you wish to know?"

"How I was made into a machine."

"I do not know that I can explain it to you. I perceive your knowledge of the nature of light is elementary. But the material with which we surrounded the space-ship in which we came, in order to protect it from the radiation of suns unknown to you, has a powerful action on all animal substances.

"It is a material not unlike your radium but a thousand times more powerful. When we reached your planet your atmosphere carried it to every part of the earth and all living things re-

ceived it. Those who were most affected by it were turned to
metal which retained that quality called 'life'. The others became merely solid metal.

"Our birds are under instructions to bring us all such individuals as possess life. In our laboratories we make their forms
over, so they will be useful to us as servants. Those who have
become solid, of course, nothing can be done for.

"We have found in the past that when we take a new planet
and make the individuals over into machines—unless we return
them to familiar surroundings they lose their reason when they
reawake. Therefore you woke in the same place in which you
passed from consciousness."

"Wonderful," said Sherman, "and where do you come from
and how did you get here?"

He felt the Lassan's amusement. "That is two questions you
have asked, not one. We come from a planet of another star,
very far away—I do not know how to express it to you. Your
methods of measurement for these things are different from
ours."

In Sherman's mind appeared a picture of the night heavens
with the tremendous ribbon of the Milky Way swinging across
its center. His attention was directed to one star, a very bright
one.

"*Rigel!*" his mind called and the thought went on. He was
suddenly transported to the neighborhood of the star, felt that
it was ages ago, long before the earth had cooled. He saw that
the star, then a sun like our own, was threatened by some
catastrophe, a titanic explosion.

Abruptly the picture was wiped out and he beheld the great
comet earthly astronomers had watched for so long before it
struck. He realized it was an interplanetary vehicle bound from
the planet of Rigel to the earth.

"But how . . ." he began to frame another question. The
Lassan cut across it firmly. "It is my turn to seek information
now. We are interested in the machine that brought you here
—the bird machine. How does it operate?"

Sherman imagined himself in the airplane's seat, operating
the controls. "But what drives it?" insisted the Lassan. "I do
not understand. No, not the queer thing at the front that turns
round. We have that principle ourselves. But the thing that
makes it turn."

For answer Sherman tried to picture the interior of the engine and show the gasoline exploding and driving it. The mind
opposite his became thoughtful at once, then flashed a question. "Are there many—explosives—in this earth?"

Sherman pictured gunpowder, dynamite and all the others
he could think of. He at once sensed that the Lassan was both
astonished and troubled. A moment later the elephant-man
rose.

"That will be sufficient for the present," he flashed and came forward to remove the helmet from Sherman's head.

A few moments later the door was swung open. Sherman saw that one of the cars was waiting for him with the word EXIT beckoning him and he was soon back in his cage.

As nearly as he could judge time he was left alone for quite twenty-four hours before being recalled for further questioning. As soon as he entered the interrogation room he perceived that something serious had engaged the attention of the Lassans. The seat was prepared for him as before but instead of one of the benches there were now three.

His acquaintance, the old Lassan, occupied the center one. On one side was a chubby elephant-man whose obesity gave a singularly infantile expression to his features and on the other a slender-limbed type as though by contrast. All three had tubes connected to the helmet which was placed on his head but he soon recognized that the older Lassan was the only one to ask questions.

"We wish to ask you about these explosives," came the message. "Are they all alike?"

"No," he answered instantly.

"What causes them to explode?"

"I am not a chemist. I don't know." The idea of chemistry was unfamiliar to them. It was apparent from their thoughts that chemistry had never occurred to them as the subject of a special study.

Then came another question. "Are there many chemists?"

An idea struck Sherman. He closed his mind against the question and flashed back the message that he came to learn as well as teach.

"That is only just. What do you wish to know?"

"What the machines are for."

"In the center of this as of every other earth lies the substance of life as it lies at the heart of every sun. The machines pierce to it and draw it up for our uses."

"What is this substance of life?"

"You would not understand if we told you. Sufficient that it is nothing known on the surface of your world. Your idea that most nearly approaches it is"—he paused, feeling about in Sherman's mind for the proper expression—"is pure light, light having material body and strength. Now let me ask—do you use explosives as we use the substance of life to fight your enemies?"

"Yes."

"What weapons do you use them in?"

Sherman thought of a revolver, then of a cannon.

"And do these weapons act at a distance?"

"Yes. May I ask a question?"

"If it is a brief one. This interview is important to us."

"How many of your people are there on the earth?"

"It is inadvisable to answer that fully but there are some hundreds. Now tell us, are there any of these weapons near this place?"

Sherman thought. West Point—Watervliet Arsenal—Iona Island, leaped into his mind. All three Lassans leaned back with a sigh of satisfaction.

Then the two younger Lassans disconnected their helmets and the older one said, "We are disposed to be generous to you. We will demonstrate one of our fighting machines to you if you will show us how to use these explosives."

There could be no particular harm in it, Sherman thought. He agreed.

The old Lassan rose. "You will retain your helmet. It is a rule that none of the lower races are allowed in the fighting machines without them and you would be unable to control one without our help."

The car carried them to the blue-domed hall where he and Marta Lami had hidden behind the shining fish. A little pang of loneliness leaped up in him at the sight. He wondered where she was and whether she had been sent back to the machines.

"No," the Lassan's thought answered his, "the other servant has been placed on other work instead. But I do not understand your idea that the other servant is somehow different from you."

"Do the Lassans then have no sex?"

"Sex? Oh, I understand. The difference between two of the lower soft races that makes reproduction possible. Our birds have it. No, we have abolished it. Our young are produced artificially."

Sixteen

They stood before the big machine. "You must do exactly as I tell you," the Lassan said. "The machinery of this instrument is very delicate. To enter you must reach up there by that fin and insert one of your fingers in the hole you will find."

As he did so Sherman saw a door, so closely fitted that when it closed there was no visible seam in the metal, swing back. They entered.

The interior of the machine was disappointingly smaller than its outside would have led one to expect. A narrow walk, railed on both sides, led down the center to the forward part. Along and slightly below this walk was a row of instrument boards not unlike those of the mining machine and at each of these one of the ape-men lay, helmet on head, apparently asleep.

"No, not asleep," the Lassan told him, "they do not require it. They have merely been thrown into a state of nothingness till we need them."

At the prow of the machine the catwalk widened into a control chamber. One of the Lassan couches was here and above it dangled a helmet which was connected with those of the slumbering ape-men. The Lassan removed the helmet he wore and exchanged it for this. Before this was another seat in which Sherman took his position.

A complex of controls surrounded him, most of them with the fingerholes which were the ordinary Lassan method of handling machinery. Directly in front of this seat was a ground-glass panel, now dark, but which lit up as soon as the Lassan had connected up his helmet to give an accurate picture of the hall in which the fighting machine stood.

"And can you see to a distance?" Sherman wondered. The answer he received was either confused or beyond his comprehension. He gathered that the four-winged birds of the Lassans acted in some way or other as their scouts, remaining in a kind of telepathic communication which the Lassan in the fighting-machine they were assigned to help.

Sherman was surprised to find how readily the enormous bulk and weight of the thing handled under the Lassan's skilled control. He understood without definitely asking that the power was furnished by that substance of life to which the Lassan had referred—in some way connected with the absolute destruction of matter.

The door swung open before them, leading them down a passage that went up for some distance, then through an immense room where some twenty more of these giants lay stored, through it and with surprising suddenness into the bright sunlight of a Catskill autumn day.

As they emerged the viewing plate swung round to show them three of the big birds whirring up from some unseen covert, spiraling into the air above them and flying level with them to form an escort.

Like most transport pilots, Sherman held a commission in the Army Reserve and had been to West Point. It was not difficult for him to guide the great fighting machine there, to find a field gun and ammunition and load it into the fighting machine.

He knew very little about artillery of any kind but when they returned to the door of the Lassan city he was enough of a mechanic to get the shell into the breech and find the firing mechanism. The gun went off with an ear-splitting crack and the shell whistled down the valley to burst against a green hillside, where they saw a graceful pine dip and fall to the shock.

At that moment such a sense of disturbance and alarm invaded Sherman's mind as he had never felt before He looked around. The Lassans who had poured out of the city to see the experiment with the gun were gathered in a tight knot. The old Lassan who was conducting him turned round abruptly.

"Into the fighting-machine at once," he commanded. "Our birds have sent a message that they are being attacked by some strange creature of your world."

As Sherman climbed through the door of the fighting machine he glanced over his shoulder to see, far down the valley a black speck against the sky.

After that it became a struggle.

Sherman found he had to be constantly on his guard, to conceal knowledge from the probing insistent mind-helmets. The Lassans seemed interested in only one subject now—human methods of making war.

Once they brought him an encyclopedia and went over every word of the articles on military subjects, questioning and cross-questioning him. Fortunately it was an old encyclopedia and he knew so little about it that in most cases he was able to throw open his mind and let his opponents see that it lay empty on these subjects.

Yet if he gave information he also received it. For little by little an understanding of the subtle material they called pure light became part of his mental equipment.

One day, as he returned from a long session in the questioning room and his cage clicked into position behind him, he was startled by a cheery strident voice.

"Well, well, if it isn't my old chum, Herbie. How's the boy?"

Sherman looked around. In the next cage was Marta Lami extending her hand through the bars.

"For Heaven's sake!" he said and took the offered hand. "How did you get here?"

"How does anyone get anywhere around this place? . . . Well, did they put the screws on you, big boy? They tried to pump me about the accident but all I'd think about was how good Broadway would look with all the lights and they didn't make much out of it."

"I'll say they put the screws on me. They've had me in there every day since, trying to find out something about guns."

"*Guns?* Ain't they got that light-ray? Wait a minute, though — You know, I think they're scared about something and I'll bet a hundred dollars against a case of full-strength Scotch I know what it is."

"Spring it. They keep pumping me and I'd like to know what it's all about."

The dancer glanced around. On the far side of her cage was an inattentive ape-man, tossing his oil-ball about. Across the corridor was another. "Come over here. They haven't put me next to you for the fun of it and they may have a dictaphone stuck around somewhere."

Obediently Sherman approached the bars of the cage.

"They put me to work making those fighting-machines," she whispered. "You know, those big shiny things like we hid behind that day we tried to make the break. They had the helmets on me most of the time because I didn't know how to use their tools and machines and I got a lot of what the guy that was running me was thinking about. He was nervous about something, and I think it was because there are some people outside going to take a whack at these babies."

"People like us?" asked Sherman.

"I don't know. I didn't get it very good but I think they're ordinary flesh-and-blood people. They came and got a lot of dopeys from the room where I lived the other day and put them in one of the new fighting-machines and took it out. It never came back. Something's up."

If the Lassans had set a device to spy on them there was no sign of it in the conversation with Sherman's interrogator during the next period. But when he saw the dancer again she beckoned him silently to her side and producing a book from one of the drawers in her lectern began to trace letters on it with a fingernail dipped in grease.

Be careful what you say, she wrote. *They know what we're talking about. They pumped me.*

He nodded. "Well, kid, what do you think? Will you ever make dancers of these Lassans?"

She giggled. "I'll say I won't. They're too slow on their pins. Rather sit still and suck up that green goo than do anything. What would I give to hear a good Latin band!"

"If I had a hand-organ now," said Sherman, "we've got the monk." He nodded toward the ape-man, while with his own fingernail he wrote, *How's chances of getting out of here? Do you know the way?*

"I'll speak to one of the big shots tomorrow," she said aloud. "Maybe we can get him to let us run a show." On the book's flyleaf appeared the words. *Only from the workroom on. It has an outside door.*

"How would I do as a dancing partner?" *Good,* he wrote. *I've doped out how to work these cars. Are you game for a try at it?*

"You haven't got the figure. I'd rather dance with that old papa Lassan that does the questions." *Sure,* she wrote, *any time you say.*

They broke off the conversation and Sherman set himself to study out a plan for escape. He had watched the cars intently both inside and out. The same needle arrangement that released the cage bars apparently actuated the mechanism of the car doors and it was located inside.

This meant that he could secure admission to the same car that carried the girl and with luck would be able to get out when she did. What to do after that was a matter of chance and inspiration.

As finally arranged between them the plan was that he was to get in the same car she did. She would tap on the back of her compartment to assure him that everything was in order, tap again when the door opened for her to get out. He would leave her a second to get her bearings, then they would make a rush for it.

He weighed the usefulness of the knife as a weapon and discarded it. But another tool, rather like a short-handled and badly shaped hammer, he did take.

At last the hour arrived. The car ran down the line of cages, paused, opened before Marta Lami's. She smiled at him, nodded, purposely delayed getting in. He fumbled desperately with his needle, fearing he could not make it. Then it went home, the little arm at the bottom of the car swung out and its door opened. As he stepped in he heard the dancer's tap of encouragement from the compartment ahead.

Evidently it was some distance to the workroom. The car made several stops on the way but at last it came—two soft knocks.

He bent, thrust home the needle. The door slid back and he stepped out into one of the blue-domed rooms. His eyes caught a maze of machinery, helmeted ape-men busy at it, beyond them the huge forms of several uncompleted fighting machines.

The dancer gripped his hand. "This way," she said, pointing along the wall past the machines. "Take it easy. Don't run till they notice us."

They made over half the distance to the door before they were spotted. Then one of the Lassans, who had sauntered over to the car stop, evidently expecting Marta, missed her and looked around. The first warning the two had was a sudden flickering of the blue lights here and there among the machines.

"Come on," shouted Marta. "There she goes!"

Sherman looked over his shoulder, saw the Lassan tugging at his pouch for a ray-gun, paused to throw one of the oil-balls, straight and true, as one pitches a baseball. It struck the elephant-man squarely between the eyes at the base of his trunk. He squealed with pain and fright and, dropping the ray-gun, ran behind the machine. For a second all the eyes in the room turned toward him. Then with another flickering of lights the hunt was up.

Sherman saw a helmeted ape-man at a machine just ahead turn slowly round, gazing vacantly, then fling himself at Marta. As she sidestepped to avoid his rush, Sherman swung a left from the heels. The metal fist took the slave flush on the jaw and down he went with a crash. The dazzling spout of a ray-gun shot past them, spattering against the wall in a shower of stars, and they had reached the exit.

"Come, oh come!" shouted Marta, tugging at the heavy door. Sherman pulled with her and at that moment another ray-gun flash struck it, just over their heads. The door gave suddenly. They tumbled through.

Into a gray twilight they struggled, shot with little dashes of rain that had beaten the valley to mud.

"No, not that way," called Sherman. "They'll look for us down the valley. Come on, up the hill."

He pulled her upward. Below and behind them came a confused rumble and they heard the great door swing open again. A burst of light, like a star in the cloudy dark, broke out and Sherman pulled the girl down behind the stump of a huge tree.

He peered cautiously round his side of the stump. In the valley beneath them, shining brilliantly in the pure white light it had released, was one of the metal fish—one smaller than usual, and without the projecting trunk.

"We've been working on them for awhile," the girl whispered. "I don't know what they're for but they aren't fighting machines."

"Wonder they don't bring the birds out," he thought. As if in answer to this idea one of the four-winged creatures strutted around the machine, blinking in the light, then took off with a whir of wings, and spiraled upward.

The light went out, reappeared as a beam pointing down the valley, and the machine moved off, slowly sweeping the sides of the hills with its pencil of illumination. He could see the multiple glow of the tubes at the stern, greenly phosphorescent, as the machine progressed. High above the bird screamed shrilly.

Seventeen

Progress up the hillside was slow; it had become completely dark. But at last in their fumbling way they reached a spot where the denudation gave place to a line of trees, looming dark and friendly overhead against the skyline and after that they went faster. They kept to the hillcrest till it ran out in a valley, then climbed the next hill, proceeding along that in the shelter of the forest. Though they necessarily went slowly they did not halt, the slip of the hill kept them from running in circles as people usually do when lost in the woods.

Just as the eastern sky began to hold some faint promise of dawn they came upon a farmhouse in a clearing at the top of a hill. It was an unprepossessing affair with a sagging roof but they burst in the door and went through it in the hope of finding weapons and perhaps an electric battery. Both were used to the bountiful electric meals of the Lassans and were beginning to feel their lack.

The best the place afforded, however, was a rather ancient axe, and a large pot of vaseline with which they anointed themselves liberally; the continued damp was making them feel rusty in the joints.

They pressed on, and did not halt to consider the situation till full day had come.

"Where do we go from here?" asked Marta, perching herself on a tree-bole.

"South, I guess," offered Sherman. "I vote for New York. If we head in there I can pick up a plane at one of the airports and fly right away from them."

"Well, it's a chance," she said. "Come on," and as they forced their way through the underbrush, "You know, from what I understood of those Lassans' thoughts, they've got something hot cooking. I'm almost sure there are other people in the world getting ready to fight them."

"Let 'em come," said Sherman. "That light-ray won't stand the chance of a whistle in a whirlwind when they get after them with heavy artillery and airplane observation."

"That's just where you're off-beam. They got a gun from somewhere and they've had all their fighting machines out, shooting it at them and then armoring up the fighting machines to stand it. And they're building guns of their own to shoot those light-bombs."

Sherman cursed himself inwardly. So that had been the result of his exchange of information with the old Lassan who was so anxious to know about guns. "How do they get away from it?" he asked.

"Well, all I know is what the guy that was controlling me thought about and let me have without knowing it.

"The outside of these fighting machines is coated with this 'substance of life' they talk about some way, so it's a perfect mirror and reflects everything that hits it, even shells. The coating reflects their light ray too but it has to have a lead backing for that. It's no good without the lead. Seems like lead will stop that light-ray every time."

"I wonder how about big guns."

"Don't know. The boss seemed to imagine the gun he had was the biggest there was."

They toiled on.

At Kingston they found a filling station and, kicking in the door, located a couple of storage batteries that supplied them with a needed meal. "What do you say to a car?" asked Sherman.

"It's running a chance, isn't it? Still, we're getting nowhere fast this way. Let's try it."

Finding a car in running order was a procedure of some difficulty and Kingston seemed a weaponless town, though Marta finally did locate one little pearl-handled .25-calibre pop-gun. Sherman eyed it dubiously.

"That's a good thing to kill mosquitoes with, but I don't think it will be much use for anything else."

"Boloney. These Lassans are yellow from way back. If I stuck this under the nose of one of them he'd throw a fit. Come on, let's go."

Eventlessly, the road flowed past under their wheels. Then, just south of Chester the dancer suddenly gripped Sherman's arm.

"What's that?" she said. "No, over there. Isn't it . . . ?"

But in one swift glance he had seen as clearly as she. Like a living thing, the car swerved from the road, dived across the ditch and, losing speed, rolled to a halt on the green lawn of a suburban bungalow. Sherman leaped out.

"Come on," he cried. "It's a fighting machine. If they've seen us they'll start shooting."

Dragging her after him he dived around the house, through a seedy flower-garden, down a path. As though to lend emphasis to his words there came the familiar buzzing roar. As Sherman dropped, pulling the girl flat on her face after him, they saw the wall of the bungalow cave in and the roof tilt slowly over and drop into the burning mass beneath. A vivid blue beam, brighter than the sunlight of the dark day, swept across the sky, winked once or twice and disappeared.

Marta would have risen but, "Take it easy," said Sherman. "If they see us they'll pop another of those tokens at us."

He wriggled along on his stomach, making for the shelter of an overgrown hedge that ran behind the next bungalow.

"Look out," called the dancer suddenly. "Here come the birds." They cowered under the shelter of the hedge and lay still scarcely daring to whisper.

The Lassan in command of the fighting machine was evidently not satisfied that he had hit them with his hasty shot. Peering through the stems they made out the shimmering form of the machine, sliding slowly past the burning house, its snout moving hither and thither questioningly. It passed through the garden, went on down the path. The bird swung to and fro over-head—nearer. Evidently it had noticed the prints their feet left in the soft ground.

"Listen, chum," said Marta Lami, "get through and find some people, then come and get me out of that hell-hole up there. If they see me they'll let you alone."

"No!" cried Sherman but she was already running out across the field. The snout of the machine lifted toward her as though to deliver a blast, then rose and discharged another beam of blue light. Sherman heard one of the birds scream in answer, saw it sweep down on soaring pinions and in a single motion snap the dancer up and away. The shimmering fighting machine swung round and turned back toward the road.

He lay still until he was sure it had gone. Then, moving carefully for fear of the terror from the skies, he crawled to the next bungalow. It yielded treasure-trove in the shape of a flashlight and a serviceable revolver. Securing a sheet from one of the beds to wrap around him as a loin-cloth he set out to trudge to New York.

After a time it occurred to him that the disaster had taken place not because they were in a car but because it had been driven unreasonably fast, and without precaution. He looked for and ultimately found another one and, keeping to the back streets and driving slowly, worked his way toward the city again.

Then another idea came to him—Newark had an airport as well as New York and it was far nearer.

Newark was a dead city; the airport was just as he had remembered it on the first day of his awakening. The little sports plane still stood on the platform, its town wing dangling. The hangars were all locked. He spent an hour or two breaking one open and when he did found nothing but a rocket-plane requiring special fuel that he did not have.

The next hangar yielded a helicopter and a trainer. He decided to chance it on the helicopter. Luckily she was full of fuel and everything seemed tight.

Not till he had it in the air did the thought of what direction he was to take occur to him. If there were a borderline along which Lassans were meeting humans in any kind of conflict it was most likely to lie southward. With this thought in mind he turned his plane to the south and, keeping the white line of foam along the coast beneath him as a guide, began to let her out.

It must have been all of an hour and three quarters later when, sharp and clear from somewhere ahead and below him, came the sound of gun-fire. There was fighting going on!

Exulting in his escape from the Lassans and that he could take their opponents information that would be of value, he swung the helicopter toward the sounds that became clearer every minute. He could see red flashes along the horizon. Down there they were locked in battle—his own people and the invaders from faraway Rigel.

Suddenly a beam of light-ray leaped from the ground. Sherman tried to loop the plane and cursed as he remembered helicopters wouldn't loop—then saw that the light was not aimed in his direction but at some object on the ground.

He banked the copter over and swung lower. Undoubtedly a Lassan fighting machine—and the beam was hitting things, things large and solid, for they collapsed under the stabbing ray. A red flame rose over the wreck. The roar of an explosion reached his ears. The battle-line!

He soared again. He must reach the headquarters of whatever men were down there.

In the darkness beneath him troops were moving. He could

catch glimpses of dark masses on the roads. Somewhere down there he distinctly heard the call of one of the four-winged birds, quite near. Then with a rush it was upon him.

He set the automatic pilot and drew his revolver, but the bird had dashed recklessly in. There was a rending screech as it came into contact with the rotor of the copter. Sherman got in one shot and then bird, man and plane tumbled toward the earth.

Eighteen

"The Lassans?" said General Grierson, looking at the sheet-clad apparition. "You mean these—mechanical monsters?"

Sherman winced. "Like myself? No, sir, those are their slaves. I thought you were familiar with them. They are elephant-men and quite different."

"I meant those long, shining objects that shoot that light-ray of theirs. Their guns shoot it out in packages but we can understand that and deal with them. Our artillery is just as good. But if we can't stop those shining things there will be no army left and that means no men left on this planet.

"All we've found that does any good so far are the twelve-inch railroad guns and we have only four of them. One was knocked out by their shells this afternoon."

"You mean their fighting-machines," Sherman replied. "I'm not absolutely certain. But I think that a shell with a lead cap would go through those machines like a knife through a piece of cheese."

There was a tiny silence in the room. Then an artillery officer said, dreamily, "The armor-piercing shells the railroad guns use have lead caps."

As though his words had released a spell there came a quick drumfire of questions. Sherman smiled. "Just a moment. One question at a time. I'm not sure I can answer them all anyway. As to what they're armored with, they have a coating of steel armor but it isn't very thick.

"It's plated on the outside with a coat of lead and outside that with the substance they call pure light. I don't know what it is but it's the same stuff they use in the light-ray and in their shells and I know that lead sheeting will stop it, even when the lead is very thin."

General Grierson swung round in his chair. "*Hartnett!* Write out an order to General Hudson, Chief Quartermaster, at once. Tell him to remove every piece of lead he can find in Atlantic City and get it melted down. Also to set up a plant for tipping all shells with lead."

Ben Ruby leaned forward. "Can we get into their city, their headquarters, or whatever they call it?"

"I hope so!" cried Sherman. "Marta Lami's in there."

"All right, young man, you'll have your chance for that," said General Grierson. "Now suppose you tell us as much as you know about these—things. Every bit of information we can get will be valuable . . .

"Oh, by the way, Hartnett. Have an order made out to the infantry to cut the points of their bullets with their knives. That will make them dum-dum and bring the lead out. Also another one to evacuate as much infantry as possible. They aren't going to be a great deal of use."

It was Ben Ruby, in a tank shining dully with the new lead plating, who led the charge against the Lassan fighting machines on the first day of the battle, who, with his little division of American tanks, had encountered three of the huge Lassan monsters outside the city. For a moment, as though dazed by the audacity of this attack, they had done nothing at all. Then all three had turned the light-rays on him.

The deadly rays glanced off, danced to the zenith in a shower of coruscating sparks and the gun of the American tank spoke —once, twice. A round hole, with a radiating star-pattern running out from it, appeared in the nose of the nearest Lassan fighting-machine and it sank to the earth like a tired animal, rolling over and over, helpless.

The other two turned to flee, swinging their long bodies around. Surrounded by shell-bursts, riddled by the lead-tipped weapons, they too struggled and sank to rise no more.

After that there had been losses, of course. The Lassan shells occasionally burst in the back areas and claimed a toll. But the advance had gone on steadily for a whole day, unchecked. The Lassans were driven back.

And then, as suddenly as they had come, they disappeared. The dodos vanished from the skies, the fighting machines from the earth. The Lassans seemed to have abandoned the struggle and retired to their underground city.

"Frankly," said Sherman, "I don't like it. Those babies may be elephants to the eye but there's nothing slow about their brains."

"General Grierson doesn't think so," said Ben Ruby. "He's all ready to hang out the flags and call it a day. He sent home two more divisions of infantry yesterday."

"General Grierson hasn't got the finest girl in the world in that hole under the Catskills, burning her fingers off," said Sherman.

"Those babies aren't licked by a million miles. Their guns are just as good as ours and that light stuff they put in them is worse than powder when it goes off. They just didn't have as many guns."

They stood on a street-corner in Philadelphia, the new head-quarters of the Army of the Federated Governments.

"Yes but what are we going to do about it?" asked Ben.

"A lot. For one thing we might get General Grierson to give us one of the laboratories here in town and some men to help us and dope out a few little presents on our side of the fence.

"I learned plenty through those thought helmets of theirs. They were so anxious to find out what I knew they didn't watch themselves."

"Nice idea," said Ben. "I know a little chemistry and between us we might put over something good. Let's go."

An hour later they were installed in their own experimental laboratory, just off Market Street, with enough assistants to help them with routine work and Gloria Rutherford and Murray Lee to keep them amused.

They talked about minor matters for a time, Ben speaking absently and cudgeling his brains for a line on which to work toward the new weapon. It is not easy to sit down and plan out a new invention without anything to start on beyond the desire to have it.

Suddenly the inner door was flung open. In the aperture they saw Sherman, his face grinning, a small piece of metal in his hand.

"I've got it, folks!" he cried. "A gravity beam!"

Nineteen

"A gravity beam!" they ejaculated together in tones varying from incredulity to simple puzzlement.

"What's that?"

"Well, it'll take quite a bit of explaining but I'll drop out the technical part of it. You see, it's like this—you remember that Einstein demonstrated that magnetism and gravity are the same thing down underneath?

"And that some of the astonomers and physicists have said that both magnetism and light are the same thing? That is, forms of vibration. Well, one of the things I picked up from the lads in this Lassan city was that light, matter, electricity, gravitation, magnetism and the whole works are the same thing in different forms.

"They've just jumped one step beyond Einstein. Now they've got a way of producing or mining pure light—that is, pure matter in its simplest form. When it's released from pressure it becomes material and raises hades all over the shop. How they get the squeeze on it I can't say. Anyway it isn't important."

"Very interesting lecture—very," commented Gloria, gravely.

"You pipe down and listen to your betters till they get through," Sherman went on. "But what I've got here is a piece of permalloy. Under certain magnetic conditions it defies gravity. Now if we can screen gravity that way, why can't we concentrate it too?"

"Why not? Except that nobody ever did it and nobody knows how," said Ben Ruby.

"Well, here's the catch. We can do anything we want to with gravity if we go about it right. What is it in chemical atoms that was weight? It's the positive charge, isn't it—the nucleus? And it's balanced by the negative charges, the electrons, that revolve around it.

"Now if we can find a way to pull some of these negative charges loose from a certain number of atoms of a substance there are going to be a whole lot of positive charges floating around without anything to bite on.

"And if we can shoot them at something it's going to have more positive charges than it can stand. And when that happens the something is going to get awful heavy. There are going to be exchanges of negative charges among all the positive charges and things are going to pop."

"Yes, yes," said Ben. "But what good does all this do?"

"Well, with what I picked up from the Lassans I think I know. They know about light and mechanics but they're rotten chemists and don't realize how good a thing they've got. Now look—if you throw a beam of radiations from a cathode tube into finely divided material you break up some of the atoms.

"Well, all we have to do is get an extra-powerful cathode tube, break up a lot of atoms and then deliver the positive charges from them onto whatever we're going for. That would be your gravity beam."

"How are you going to get radiation powerful enough to split up enough atoms to do you any good?" inquired Ben.

"Easy—use a radium cathode. The Lassans have the stuff but never think of using it. They think it's a by-product in their pure-light mines and just play around with it."

"Mmm, sounds possible," said Ben. "That is, in theory. I'd like to see it work in practice. How are you going to throw this beam?"

"Cinch. Down a beam of light. Light will conduct sound or radio waves even through a vacuum and this stuff I'm sending isn't so very different. Whatever we hit will act as an amplifier and spread the effect through the whole body."

"Boy, you want to be careful you don't blow up the earth," said Murray Lee. "Well, Gloria, I guess we're indicated to go out and dig up some radium. Let's fool them by going before they ask us. There ought to be a supply in some of the hospitals. I thought we'd lost all chance of using atomic power—but it looks as if we may get it back in a simpler way."

It was the next evening before Murray and Gloria got back to the laboratory. The device they now saw was mounted on a stand, with long ropes of electrical connections running back from it, and had been pushed back to the end of the room. Opposite it was another stand with a two-foot-square piece of sheetiron resting on a chair in its center. The lens of a big camera was pointed in that direction.

"Now," said Sherman, "watch your uncle and see what happens."

He turned a switch. The tube at the back of the apparatus lit up with a vivid violet glow and a low humming sound filled the room.

"I decided to use powdered lead in the box," he explained. "It is the heaviest metal available and gives us the largest number of nuclei to project."

A second switch was thrown in and a beam of light leaped from the camera and struck in the center of the iron sheet, producing merely a mild white illumination.

"Poof!" said Gloria. "That isn't suchamuch. I could do that with a flashlight."

"Right you are. I haven't let her go yet. Hold your breath now."

He bent over, drove a plunger home. For just a second the only visible effect was a slight intensification of the beam of light. Then there was a report like a thunderclap. A dazzling ball of fire appeared on the stand; a cloud of smoke, and Murray and Gloria found themselves sitting on the floor.

The iron plate had completely vanished. So had the chair, all but two of its legs, which, lying in the center of the stand, were burning brightly. The acrid odor of nitrogen dioxide filled the room.

"Golly!" said Ruby, seizing a fire extinguisher from the wall and turning it on the blaze. "That's even more than we expected. Look, it made a hole right through the wall! We'll have to keep that thing tied up."

"I'll say you will," said Murray, helping Gloria up. "It's as bad for the guy that's using it as the one at the other end. Seriously you've got something good there. What happened to the iron plate?"

"Disintegrated. Let's see, where does iron come in the periodic table, Ben? Twenty-six? Then you'll probably find small quantities of all the chemical elements from twenty-five down in that heap of ashes. Phooey, what a rotten smell! That must be the action of the beam on the nitrogen in the air."

"There's a lot to be worked out in this thing yet, though," declared Ben, "and precious little time in which to work it out.

"For one thing, we've got to get a searchlight that will throw a narrow pencil of light for a long distance. I don't think those elephant-men are going to let us poke this thing under their noses. And for another we've got to dope out something to keep it in and some way to furnish current for it."

"Can't you work it from a tank?" asked Murray, "and rig up a friction accumulator to work from the tracks?"

"I can but I don't like the idea," Sherman replied. "From the way those Lassans took to our airplanes I could make a guess that when they come they're going to come in some kind of flying machine. The dodos are no good in modern war. We'd never catch any kind of an airplane with a tank."

"Say, you guys have less ingenuity for a couple of inventors than anyone I ever heard of," Gloria put in. "Why don't you get one of these Australian rocket-planes and fix it up? It's big enough to hold all your foolishness and if this thing is half as powerful as it looks, you ought to be able to harness it some way for a power-plant. Then you can plaster your rocket all over with armor. I think . . ."

Sherman interrupted her by bringing his fist down on the table with a bang that made the glasses rattle.

"You've *got* it! With the punch this thing gives us used as a rocket we'd have power enough to fly to the moon if we wanted to. Let's go."

It was another week before workmen, even toiling with all the machine-shop facilities of Philadelphia at their disposal and working day and night, could turn out the machine to Sherman's design. It was two more before the apparatus was installed. The trial trip was set for the early morning when there would be least chance of atmospheric disturbance.

The *Monitor*—she had been named for the famous fighting craft with which the American navy ushered in a new age in the history of war—now stood near the center of the flying field at the Philadelphia airport—a long, projectile-like vessel with gleaming metal sides, set with heavy windows, ten feet in diameter and nearly twice as long.

At her stern a funnel-like opening led to the interior. This was the exhaust for the power-plant. At her bow the sharp nose was blunted off and its tip was occupied by the lens of a high-powered parabolic searchlight, slightly recessed and with the discharge tubes for the atomic nuclei arranged around its edge so they would be thrown directly into the light-beam as soon as generated.

As the four approached her she had been placed on the ramp from which she was to start, slanting slightly upward, with a buffer of timber and earth behind it to take up the enormous recoil her power plant was expected to develop.

"How do you get in?" asked Gloria, walking around the *Monitor* and discovering no sign of a door.

"Oh, that's a trick I borrowed from our friends the Lassans," explained Sherman. "Look here." He led her to a place halfway along one side, where two almost imperceptible holes marred the shining brightness of the new vessel's sides. "Stick your fingers in."

She did as directed, pressed and a wide door in the side of the projectile swung open. "Bright thought. No handles to break off."

They stepped in, bending their heads to avoid the low ceiling.

"She isn't as roomy or comfortable or as heavily armored as the one I mean to build later," explained Sherman, "but this is only an experimental craft, built in a hurry, so I had to take what I could get.

"Now here, Murray, you sit here. Your job is going to be to mind the gravity beam that furnishes us our power. Every time you get the signal from me you throw this power switch. That will turn on all three switches at the stern and shoot the gravity beam out for the exhaust.

"You see, we can't expect to keep up a steady stream of explosions with this kind of a machine. We wouldn't be able to control it. We'll travel in a series of short hops through the air, soaring between hops like a glider."

"How are you going to soar without wings?" asked Murray.

"We have wings. They fold into the body at the back. I've made them automatic. When the power switch is thrown the wings fold in. After the explosion they come out automatically unless we disconnect them. If we want to really go fast we'll disconnect them and go through the air like a projectile."

"Oh, I see. Will the windows stand the gaff?"

"I hope to tell you they will. I had them made of fused quartz, with an outer plating of leaded glass, just in case the Lassans try to get fresh with that light-ray of theirs.

"Now, Gloria, you sit here. You're the best shot in the crowd and it's going to be your job to run that searchlight in the prow. As soon as you pick up anything with it Ben will throw his switch and whatever is at the end of it will get a dose of pure protons.

"We'll have to do a good deal of our aiming by turning the ship itself. I made the searchlight as flexible as I could but I couldn't get a great deal of turn to it on account of the necessity of getting the nuclei into the light beam."

"By the way," asked Murray. "Won't this pure light armor of the Lassans knock your beam for a row of ashcans?"

"I should say not! If they use it we've got 'em. That stuff has weight and the minute this beam of ours hits it it will intensify the effect. No matter how much pressure they have on it it will blow up all over the place. All set? Let's go. Throw in your switch, Murray."

Murray did as directed. There was a humming sound and the

tiny beam of light leaped across the rear end of the ship and out the exhaust. Across it fell a thin powder of iron filings—the material that was to be decomposed to furnish the power.

With a roar, the *Monitor* leaped forward, throwing all of them back into their heavily padded seats, then dipped and soared as the wings came into play. The passengers glanced through the windows. Beneath them the outskirts of Philadelphia were already speeding by.

"Say," said Ben, "this is some bus. We must be making eight hundred miles an hour."

"Sure," said Sherman. "We could do over seventeen hundred as a pure projectile but we can't use that much speed and keep our maneuvering power."

Twenty

"Where to, folks?" asked Sherman, during one of their periods of soaring, as they floated high above the hilly country to the west of the Delaware River.

"Oh, most anywhere," said Ben. "I'd like to see you try out this new-fangled gun of yours on something though."

"What shall we try it on—a house?"

"No, that's too easy. We saw what it could do to things like that in the laboratory. Find a nice rock."

"Okay, here goes. Don't give her the gun for a minute, Murray."

With wings extended the *Monitor* spiraled down toward the crest of the mountain. A projecting cliff stood just beneath them, sharply outlined in the rays of the morning sun.

"Now this is going to be difficult," warned Sherman. "Throw that connecting bar, Ben. It holds the power-switch and the beam-switch together so they're both turned on at once. Otherwise the recoil we'd get on this end of the beam would tumble us over backward. Hold it while I set the controls. We've got to take a jump as soon as we fire or we'll pop right into the mess we make. Ready? All right, Gloria, go ahead with your searchlight."

The beam of the searchlight shot out, pale in the daylight, wavered a second, then outlined the crest of the cliff.

"*Shoot!*" cried Sherman.

There was a terrific report—a shock—the *Monitor* leaped, quivering in every part, and as they spiraled down to see what damage they had done they beheld no cliff at all but a rounded cup at the tip of the mountain in which a mass of molten rock boiled and simmered.

"Fair enough," said Ben. "I guess that will do for the Lassans, all right. Home, James?"

"Right," answered Sherman. "We've found out all we want to know this trip."

The homeward journey was accomplished even more swiftly than the trip northward. As they glided slowly to earth at the airport a little group of officers was waiting to meet them.

"What in thunder have you been doing?" one of them greeted the Americans. "Your static or whatever it was you let loose burned out all the tubes in half the army radio sets in New Jersey."

"By the nine gods of Clusium!" said Sherman. "I never thought of that. We're reducing matter pretty much to its lowest terms and it's all a good deal alike on that scale—vibrations that may be electricity, magnetism, light or matter.

"Of course, when we let go that shot there was enough radiation to be picked up on Mars. I'll have to figure out a way to get around that. Those Lassans are no bums as electricians and after we've been at them once or twice they'll be able to pick up our radiation whenever we're coming and duck us."

"There's another thing," said Ben. "I thought the *Monitor* vibrated a good deal when you let that shot go."

"It did. We'll have to get more rigidity or we'll be shaking ourselves to pieces every time we shoot. But this, as I said, is an experimental ship. What we've got to do now is turn in and build a real one with heavy armor and a lot of new tricks."

It was two days later when they stood at headquarters on the flying field again. The *Monitor* had made three more trips, on one of them flying over the Lassan city without seeing anything more important than the Australian signal station perched on a nearby hill.

Meanwhile the Army of the Federated Governments had pushed out its tentacles, searching the barren waste that had been the most fruitful country in the world. East, west, south and north the report was the same—no sign of the Lassans or any other living thing.

"I wish," said Gloria, "that those lads would stick their noses out. I'd like to try the *Monitor* on them."

"You'll get all you want of that," said Ben a trifle grimly.

"Wait a minute," called an officer at a desk as a telegraph key began tapping. "This looks like something." He translated the dots and dashes for them.

"Lassan—city—door—opening . . . it's from the signal station on that mountain right over it . . . Big—ball—coming out—will—will— What's this? The message seems to end." He depressed the key vigorously and waited. It remained silent.

"Oh boy!" said Sherman. "There she goes! They got that signal station, I'll bet a dollar to a ton of Lassan radiation."

The officer was hammering the key again. "We're sending out airplane scouts now," he said. "Too bad about the signal station but that's war!"

"Come on, gang," said Ben. "Let's get out to the flying field. Looks like we're going to be in demand."

In a car borrowed from the headquarters staff they raced out to the field where the *Monitor* stood, ready on its ramp for any emergency. Just as they arrived an airplane became visible, approaching from the north. It circled the field almost as though the pilot were afraid to land, then dipped and came to a slow and hesitating stop.

The onlookers noticed that its guy wires were sagging, its wheels uneven. It looked like a wreck of a machine which had not been flown for ten years, after it had lain in some hangar where it received no attention at all.

As they ran across the field toward it, the pilot climbed slowly out. They noticed that his face was pale and horror-struck, his limbs shaking.

"All gone," he cried to the oncoming group.

"What? Who? What's the matter?"

"Everything. Guns—tanks—planes! The big ball's got 'em. Almost got—" He collapsed in Ben's arms in a dead faint.

"Here," said Ben, handing the unconscious flyer to one of the Australian officers. "Come on, there's something doing up there. Big ball, eh? Well, we'll make a football of it. That chap looks as though he'd been through a milling machine, though. The Lassans certainly must have something good."

With a shattering crash as Murray Lee gave her all the acceleration she would take, the *Monitor* left the ramp, soared to gain altitude and headed north, amid a chorus of explosions.

In less than five minutes the thickly-settled districts of northern New Jersey were flowing by beneath them.

"Wish we had some radio in this bus," remarked Ben Ruby. "We could keep in touch with what's going on."

"It would be convenient," said Sherman, "but you can't have everything. The Lassans aren't going to wait for us to work out all our problems. Look—over there!"

At nearly the same level as themselves and directly over the city of Newark a huge globular object, not unlike an enormous green cantaloupe, appeared to float in the air. From its underside a thin blue beam of some kind of ray reached the ground. From the face turned diagonally away from them a paler wider beam, yellowish in color, reached down toward the buildings of the city.

Where it fell on them they collapsed in shattering ruin—roofs piled on walls, chimneys tumbled to the ground. There was no flame, no smoke, no sound—just that sinister monster moving slowly along, demolishing the city of Newark almost as though it were by an effort of thought.

"Hold tight, everybody," cried Sherman. "Going up."

The *Monitor* slanted skyward. Through the heavy quartz of her windows they could see a battery of field guns, cleverly concealed behind some trees in the outskirts of the city, open fire. At the first bursts the monster globe swung slowly round, the pale yellow ray cutting a swath of destruction as it moved. The shells of the second burst struck all around and on it. "Oh, good shooting!" cried Gloria but even as she spoke the yellow ray bore down and the guns became silent.

"What have they got?" she shouted between the bursts of the *Monitor's* rocket motor.

"Don't know," replied Sherman, "but it's good. Ready? Here goes. Cut off, Murray."

From an altitude of 15,000 feet the *Monitor* swept down in a long curve. As she dived Gloria swung the searchlight beam toward the green globe.

"Go!" shouted Sherman and Ben threw the switch. There was a terrific explosion, the *Monitor* pitched wildly, then, under control, swung round and began to climb again. Through the thinning cloud of yellow smoke, they could see a long black scar across the globe's top with lines running out from it like the wrinkles on an old old face.

"*Blast!*" said Sherman. "Only nicked him. They must have something good in the line of armor on that thing. Look how it stood up. Watch it, everybody, we're going to go again, Gloria!"

Again the searchlight beam swung out and down, sought the green monster. But this time the Lassan globe acted more quickly. The yellow ray lifted, probed for them, caught them in its beam. Instantly the occupants of the *Monitor* felt a racking pain in every joint. The camera-boxes of the gravity-beam trembled in their racks. The windows, set in solid steel though they were, shook in their frames. The whole body of the rocket-ship seemed about to fall apart.

Desperately Sherman strove with the controls—dived, dodged then finally, with a raised hand to warn the rest, side-slipped and tumbled toward the earth, pulling out in a swinging curve with all power on—a curve that carried them a good ten miles away before the yellow ray could find them.

"Boy!" said Murray Lee, feeling of himself. "I feel as though every joint in my body were loose. What was that, anyway?"

"Infra-sound," replied Sherman. "You can't hear it but it gets you just the same. Like a violinist and a glass. He can break it if he hits the right note. They must have found a way to turn that pure light of theirs into pure sound and vibrate it on every note of the scale all at once besides a lot the scale never heard of. Well, now we know."

"Do we go back and take another whack at them?" asked Murray Lee.

"I don't like to do it with this ship," Sherman replied. "If we had the *Monitor Two* it would be easy. With that extra vacuum chamber around her, she'll take quite a lot of that infra-sound racket. Vacuum doesn't conduct sound you know, though we'd

get some of it through the struts. But this one— Still I suppose
we'll have to show them we mean business."

The *Monitor* turned, pointed her lean prow back toward Newark and bore down. In their flight from the infra-sound ray the
Americans had dived behind a fluffy mass of low-hanging cloud.
As they emerged from it, they could see the huge green ball,
far up the river, retreating at its best speed.

"Aha," Sherman said. "He doesn't like gravity beams. Well,
come on, give her the gun, Murray."

Under the tremendous urge of the gravity-beam explosions
at her tail, the *Monitor* shot skyward, leaving a trail of orange
smoke in her wake as the beam decomposed the air where it
struck it. Sherman lifted her behind the clouds, held the course
for a moment, called "Ready, Gloria?" and then dropped.

Like a swooping hawk, the *Monitor* plunged from her hiding
place. Sherman had guessed right. The green ball was not five
miles ahead of them, swinging over the summits of the Catskills
to reach its home. As they plunged down the yellow ray came
on, stabbed quickly, once, twice, thrice—caught them for a
brief second of agonizing vibration, then lost them again as Sherman twisted the *Monitor* around.

Then Gloria's beam struck the huge globule fair and square.
Ben Ruby threw the switch and a terrific burst of orange flame
swallowed the whole center of the Lassan monster.

Prepared though they were for the shock, the force of the
explosion threw the ship out of control. It gyrated frantically,
spinning up, down and sidewise as Sherman worked the stick.
The Catskills reared up at them, shot past in a whirl of greenery.
Then with a splash they struck the surface of the Hudson.

Fortunately, the *Monitor's* wings were extended and took up
most of the shock at the cost of being shattered against her
sides. Through the beam-hole at the stern the water began to
flow into the interior of the ship.

"Give her the gun!" called Sherman frantically, working his
useless controls. There was a report, a shock, a vivid cloud of
steam. Ripping and coughing like a child that has swallowed
water in haste, the *Monitor* rose from the stream, her broken
wings trailing behind her.

"I don't know whether I can fly this crate or not," said Sherman, trying to make what was left of the controls work. "Shoot,
Murray—if we put on enough power we won't have to soar."

There was a renewed roar of explosions from the *Monitor*.
Desperately, swinging in a wide curve that carried her miles out
of her way, she turned her nose southwards.

"Make Philly," cried Sherman cryptically above the sound of
the explosions that were driving their craft through the air at
over nine hundred miles an hour. Almost as he said it they saw
the airport beneath them. The *Monitor* swerved erratically. The
explosions ceased. She dived, plunged and slithered to a racking

stop across the foreshore of the seaplane port, ending up with a crash against a float, and pitched all four occupants from their seats onto the floor.

"Well, that's one for you and one for me," said Sherman as he surveyed the wreckage. "We used up that green ball all right but the old *Monitor* will never pop another one. Did anyone notice whether there were any pieces left by the way?"

"I did," said Gloria. "As we came up out of the water I could see a few hunks lying around on the hill."

"Mmm," remarked Sherman, "they must be built pretty solidly. Wish I knew what was in them. You gave her all the power we had, didn't you?"

"There's something else I'd like to know," said Ben. "And that's whether they had time to warn the rest of the Lassans what they were up against. If they did we stand a chance. The way I have these guys figured is that they're good but they don't like to fight unless they're sure of winning. If I'm right we'll have time to get *Monitor Two* into commission and before they come out again we'll be ready for them."

"Yes, and on the other hand, if they did have time to warn them, they'll sit down and dope out some new trick. Though I have a hunch they won't find an answer to that gravity-beam so easily."

Twenty-One

The little group separated, going about their several tasks. Whatever the cause Ben proved to be right about the Lassan green spheres. After that one brief incursion, in which they had wrecked the greater part of Newark and most of the artillery the Australians had established to bear on the door of the Lassan city, they seemed to have returned to their underground home, realizing that the earthmen still had weapons the equal of anything the creatures of Rigel could produce.

For a whole week there was no sign of them. Meanwhile the Federated Army dug itself in and prepared for the attack that was now believed certain. The success of the first *Monitor* had been great enough, it was decided, to warrant the construction of more than one of the second edition. General Grierson wished to turn the whole resource of the Allied armies to building an enormous number but under Ben's persuasion he consented to concentrate on five.

For, as Ben pointed out to the general, the training of flesh-and-blood men for these craft would be labor lost.

"They couldn't stand the acceleration that will be necessary, for one thing. With *Monitor Two* we expect to be able to work up swiftly to over a thousand miles an hour and the most acceleration a flesh-and-blood man can stand won't give us that speed quickly enough.

"Of course, we could make 'em so they worked up speed slowly but then they wouldn't be able to cut down fast enough to maneuver. And for another thing this infra-sound ray the Lassans project would kill a flesh-and-blood man the first time it hit him. What we need for this kind of war is supermen in the physical sense.

"I don't want to make any such snooty statements as that Americans are better than other people but we happen to be the only ones who have undergone this mechanical operation and we're the only people in the world who can stand the gaff. You'll just have to let us make out the best we can. In fact, it might be better for you to re-embark the army and let us fight it out all alone. The more women we have here, the more we'll have to protect."

The general had been forced to agree to the first part of this statement but he gallantly refused to abandon the Americans though he did send away men, troops and guns which had become useless in this new brand of warfare.

Even as it stood there were only fourteen of the mechanical Americans remaining—enough to man three of the monitors.

But one day as *Monitor II*, shining with newness, stood on her ramp having the searchlights installed, Herbert Sherman came dashing across the flying field, waving a sheet of paper.

"I've got it," he cried, "I've got it! I knew I got something from those Lassans about electricity that I hadn't known before and now I know what it is. Look!"

"Radar?" queried Ben.

"No, read it," said Sherman. "Radar's out. But this is a thousand times better."

He extended the sheet to Ben, who examined the maze of figures gravely for a moment.

"Now suppose you interpret," he said. "I can't read Chinese."

"Sap. This is the formula for the electrical device I was talking about."

"Yeh. Well, go on, spill it."

"Well, in our black box, we've been breaking up the atoms of lead into positive and negative charges. We've been using the positive and then just turning the negative loose. This thing will make use of both and give us a swell new weapon all at once.

"Look—the negative charges will do for our gravity beam just as well as the positive. They will create an excess of negative electrons instead of an excess of positive protons in the object we hit and cause atomic disintegration. It's a gravity process just the same but a different one. Now that gives us something else to do with the positives.

"You know what a Leyden jar is? One of those things you charge with electricity, then you touch the tip and bang—you get a shock. Well, this arrangement will make a super-Leyden jar of the *Monitor*. Every time she fires the gravity-beam the positive charges will be put into her hull and she'll soon be able to load up with a charge that will knock your eye out when it's let loose."

"How's that? I know the outside of the *Monitor* is covered with lead and so is the outside of a Leyden jar but what's the connection?"

"Well, it's this way—when you load up a Leyden jar the charge is not located in the plating but in the glass. Now the *Monitor* has a lot of steel, which will take up the charge just as well as glass. As soon as she fires the gravity-beam these filaments will load her up with the left-over positives till she grunts. See?"

"And since the earth is building up a lot of negative potential all the time, all you have to do is get your bird between you and the earth and then let go at him?"

"That's the idea. It'll make an enormous spark-gap and whatever is between us and the earth will get the spark. Sock them with a flash of artificial lightning. We'll use the light-beam as a conductor just as with the gravity-beam."

"Sounds good but I want to see the wheels go round. How much of a potential do you think you can build up in the *Monitor?*"

"Well, let's see. We've got two thicknesses of nine-inch steel —volts to a cubic inch—by cubic inches. Holy smoke, look how this figures out—over eleven million volts!

"That's theory, of course. There'll be some leakage in practice and we won't have time to build up that much negative potential every time we shoot. If we only do half that well we'll have a pretty thorough-going charge of lightning. Peterson, come over here. I want you to make some changes on this barge."

Monitor II stood on the ramp that had once held her elder sister, her outer coating of lead glimmering dully in the morning sun. Here and there, along her shining sides were placed the windows through which her crew would watch the progress of the battle.

Her prow was occupied by the same type of searchlight the earlier *Monitor* had borne. But this time the searchlight was surrounded by a hedge of shining silver points—the discharge mechanism for the lightning flash. At the stern, instead of the opening running right through into the ship, was a tight bulkhead, with the connections for the gravity-beam rocket-mechanism leading through it.

As Sherman pointed out, "If this lightning is going to do us any good we've got to get above our opponent and those Lassans have built machines that made interplanetary voyages. We've got to make this boat airtight so that we can go right after them as far as Rigel if necessary."

It had been decided, in view of the other monitors they were building, to make the trial trip of the second rocket-cruiser also a training voyage, with Beeville and Yoshio replacing Murray Lee and Gloria in her crew.

They climbed in. The spectators stood back and with a thunderous rush of explosions and a cloud of yellow gas the second *Monitor* plunged into the blue.

"Where shall we go?" asked Sherman as the ship swooped over the plains of New Jersey.

"How much speed is she making?" asked Ben Ruby.

"I don't know exactly. We didn't have time to invent and install a reliable gauge. But . . ." He glanced at the map before him, then down through the windows at the surrounding country . . . "I should say not far short of a thousand an hour. I'm not giving her all she'll stand, even yet."

"If you've got that much speed why don't you visit Chicago?" asked Beeville. "The Australians have only pushed as far as Ohio and there may be some people there."

"Bright thought," remarked Sherman, swinging the prow of the vessel westward.

For some time there was silence in the cabin as the rocket-ship, with alternate roar and swoop, pushed along. Yoshio was the first to speak. "Ah, gentlemen, I observe beneath window trace of city of beer, formerly Cincinnati."

"Sure enough," said Ben, peering down. "There doesn't seem to be much beer there now, though."

The white city of the Ohio vanished beneath them, silent and deserted, no sign of motion in its dead streets.

"You know," said Sherman, "sometimes when I see these cities and think of all the Lassans have wrecked it gives me an ache. What right did they have to come to earth anyway? We were letting them alone."

"Same right wolf obtains when hungry," said Yoshio. "Wolf is larger than rabbit—end of rabbit."

"Oh, I don't know," said Ben Ruby, "it may be a good thing for the old world at that. You never heard of *all* the governments of the world cooperating before as they are now, did you? There are still people alive you know. Civilization hasn't been killed off by a long shot.

"And that blue coloring that affected all the people who didn't get metalized isn't going to be permanent. The babies being born there now are normal, I hear. In a few generations the earth will be back to where it was except for us. I don't know of any way to reverse this metal evolution."

"Neither do I," said Beeville, "unless we can get another dose of the 'substance of life' as the Lassans call it—and we won't get that unless they decide to leave the earth in a hurry."

"Look," said Sherman, "there's Chicago now. But what's that? No, there—along the lake front."

Following the direction of his pointing finger they saw something moving vaguely along Lake Shore Boulevard, something that might be a car—or a man!

"Let's go down and see," offered Ben.

The explosions were cut off, the wings extended, and Sherman spiraled carefully downward to the spot where they had seen the moving object. With the nicety of a magician he brought the ship to a gliding stop along the park grass. Followed by the rest Ben Ruby leaped out. The edge of the drive was a few yards away. As they emerged from the ship no one was visible but as they walked across the grass, a figure, metallic like themselves, and with a gun in one hand, stepped from behind a tree.

"Stand back!" it warned. "Who are you and what do you want?"

"Conversation with sweet-looking gentleman," said Yoshio politely, with a bow.

"Why, we're members of the American air force," said Ben, "cooperating with the Federated Armies against the Lassans, and we were on an exploring expedition to see if we could find any more Americans."

"Oh," said the figure. "All right then. Come on out, boys."

From behind other trees in the little park a group of metallic figures, all armed, rose into sight.

"My name's Ben Ruby," said Ben, extending his hand, "at present General commanding what there is of the American army."

"Mine's Slasinger. I suppose you could call me Mayor of Chicago since those birds got Lindstrom. So you're fighting the Lassans, eh? Good. We'd like to take a few pokes at them ourselves but that light-ray they have is too much for us. All we can do is pot the birds."

"Oh," said Ben, "we've got that beat and a lot of other stuff too. How many of you are there?"

"Eight including Jones, who isn't here now."

The explanations went on. It appeared that Chicago, St. Louis and other western cities had been overwhelmed as had New York—the same rush of light from the great comet, the same unconsciousness on every side, the same awakening and final gathering together of the few individuals who had been fortunate enough to attract the attentions of the Lassans' birds and so be sent to their cities for transformation into Robots.

Since that time the birds had raided Chicago and the other western cities unceasingly and had reduced the original company of some thirty-odd to the eight individuals Ben had encountered. Before the birds had attacked them, however, they had managed to get a telegraph wire in operation and learn that people were alive at Los Angeles—whether mechanized or not they were uncertain but they thought not.

Once, several weeks before, a Lassan fighting-machine had passed through the city, wrecked a few buildings with the light-ray and disappeared westward as rapidly as it had come.

With some difficulty and a good deal of crowding the eight Chicagoans were got into the *Monitor II* for the return journey. They were a most welcome reinforcement and would furnish enough Americans to man all five of the extra rocket-cruisers.

"I hope," remarked Sherman, a couple of days later, "that those Lassans don't come out quite yet. We've got the ships to meet them now but the personnel isn't as well trained as I should like. Slasinger nearly smashed up one of the ships yesterday making his landing and one of the wings on another cracked up this morning when Roberts tried to turn too short. These rocket-ships are so fast you need a whole state to handle them in."

"And I," replied Ben Ruby, "hope they come out soon. As you say, we've got the ships now but they're not so slow themselves. With the building methods they have they can turn out ships faster than we can."

"All the same I'd like a few days more," Sherman countered. "And I have another idea. I think we ought to keep at least one monitor on patrol over the Lassan city all the time. They're apt to get out and sneak one over on us. She can stay high up in the stratosphere.

"Of course, she can't radio, but she can fire a couple of shots if she sights them coming out and we can make a static detector that will register the disturbance. Then we can catch them as fast as they come out when they'll be easiest to attack."

"How about the other Lassan city out in the Black Hills?" asked Ben.

"It would be bad strategy to try to handle them both at once, wouldn't it?" said Sherman. "Still, if you think so. . . ."

Twenty-Two

It was *Monitor VII* manned by the Chicagoans, which had the honor of sighting the enemy. Just as the twilight of a bright May day was closing down over the radar men at the Philadelphia airport, the static detector marked an unusual disturbance, then two quick shocks, which must have come from the patrol's bow beam. In quick succession, the other five, standing ready on their starting ramps, took in their crews, and roared up and away in a torrent of explosions at a thousand miles an hour.

Soaring to fifty thousand feet above the earth the squadron of rocket ships made its way north, *Monitor II* in the lead.

"Well, here we go," called Gloria from her seat behind the searchlight. "Hope they don't give us the runaround this time."

"They won't have the chance," said Ben. "That is, provided those Chicago boys have sense enough to remember their instructions and let them alone till we all get there. With six of these ships we ought to be able to rough 'em up a little bit."

At a speed of over a thousand miles an hour, thanks to the thinness of the atmosphere through which they were traveling, it was only a few minutes' hop from Philadelphia to the Catskill city of the elephant-men. Ben had hardly finished speaking before Sherman called from the control seat, "There they are!"

Far beneath, half-revealed, half-ridden by the few tiny clouds of fleece that hung at the lower altitudes they could see the naked scar in the hills that marked the Lassan headquarters. Around it floated half a dozen of the huge green balls they had encountered on the last occasion.

As they swept by, another one, looking like a grape at the immense distance, trundled slowly out from the enormous door, swung to and fro for a second or two, then swam up to join those already in the sky. *Monitor VII* was to the north and above them—as she perceived the American fleet she swept down to join the formation, falling into her prearranged place.

"Do we go now?" asked Sherman.

"Not yet," said Ben. "Give them all a chance to get out. I hope they intend to fight it out to a finish this time."

They turned north, giving the Lassans time to assemble. "What's the arrangement?" asked Gloria. "Do we all go for them at once?"

"No. We dive in first and the rest follow behind, pulling up before they get in range. If anything happens to us they'll rescue us—if they can. You see we don't know what they've got any more than they know what we've got and I thought it would be a good idea to try the first attack with only one ship. In a pinch the rest can get away—if the Lassans haven't developed a lot of speed on those green eggs of theirs."

"How many now?" asked Sherman, from the controls.

"Two—five—nine—eleven—oh, I can't count them all," said Gloria. "They keep changing formation so. There's a lot of them and they're coming up toward us, but slowly. They haven't got that blue beam at the base any more either—you know the one that globe we got after was riding on."

As they approached it was indeed evident that the green globes were rising slowly through the twilight in some kind of loose formation. It was too complex for the American observers to follow in the brief glimpses they were vouchsafed as they swept past at hurricane speed.

There seemed to be dozens of the Lassan globes—as though they expected to overwhelm opposition by mere force of numbers. Nearer and nearer came the rocketships, nearer and nearer loomed the sinister Lassan globes, betraying no signs of life, silent and ominous.

"Go?" called Sherman from his seat at the controls.

"Go!" said Ben.

The *Monitor II* dived. As she dived Gloria Rutherford switched on the deadly beam of the searchlight which would carry the gravity-beam against their enemies. For a moment it sought the green globes, then caught one fairly. Ben Ruby threw the switch and down the light beam leaped the terrible stream of the broken atoms like a wave of death. Leaped—and failed!

For as it struck the green globe, instead of the rending explosion and the succeeding collapse, there came only a bright handful of stars, a coruscating display of white fire that dashed itself around the Lassan ship like foam on some coastrock. It reeled backward, driven from its position under the tremendous shock but remained intact.

"Well, I'm a son-of-a-gun!" declared Sherman as he put the *Monitor* into a spiral climb at nine hundred miles an hour to avoid any counter-attack. "If they haven't found a screen! I didn't think it was possible. Goes to show you you never can tell, especially with the Lassans. Look out folks, here comes the gaff. I'm going to loop!"

For as he spoke the formation of green globes had opened out—swiftly by ordinary standards though slowly in comparison with the frantic speed of the American rocket-vessel. From half a dozen of them the racking yellow ray of infrasound leaped forth to seek the audacious ship that had attacked them single-handed.

All round her they stabbed the atmosphere, striking the few clouds and driving them apart in a fine spray of rain but missing the *Monitor* as she twisted and heaved at frantic speed.

Twenty miles away and high in the air they pulled up to recover themselves.

"And *that*," Sherman went on with his interrupted observation, "explains why they aren't using those blue beams for support any more. Of course a gravity screen that would work against our beam would work against the gravity of the earth just as well. They must have some way of varying its effect though. They aren't rising very fast and haven't got much speed."

"Probably they can't stand the acceleration," suggested Murray.

"Probably you're right. They can't have less than one Lassan in each globe. Of course, they might control them by radio with the thought-helmets and have the crews all robots but that wouldn't be a Lassan way of doing things.

"And I doubt if they'd think radio safe, even if they know about it, of which I'm not sure. We're shedding any amount of static around, and would play merry hell with most any radio. Wish I knew how they worked that gravity screen, though. I'll bet a boatload of *Monitors* against a thought-helmet that it's magnetic."

"Wish we had some way to signal the rest of the fleet," said Ben as they swung into their position at the head of the formation again. "I don't want them pushing in there with the gravity-beam if it isn't going to do any good."

Murray laughed. "They'll find it out soon enough. I think we've got plenty of speed to beat those infra-sound rays too. If that's as strong as they come we've got 'em licked."

"Don't crow yet, chum," said Gloria. "You don't know what those babies have up their sleeves—excuse me, their trunks."

As the American fleet formed for a mass attack the Lassan globes had been rising and now they were a bare five thousand feet below the rocket-cruisers, swinging along at a height of 25,000 feet above the earth in the last rays of the setting sun. As the green globes rose they took their places in a formation like an enormous crescent, the ends of which were extended as each new globe came up to join it.

"Looks like they want to get us in the middle and pop us from all directions at once," observed Sherman. "Well, here goes. Pick the end of the line—that's our best chance. How's your potential, Gloria?"

"Okay, chief," she answered. "Lightning this time?"

He nodded. The rockets of the *Monitor II* roared. Its prow dipped forward and at an incredible speed it swept down on the line of Lassan warships, followed by the rest of the American fleet. But it was no surprise this time. As the monitors plunged in, from every green globe that could bring them to bear, the long yellow rays shot forth.

Right through them the *Monitor II* plunged. The grate of it, even through their double coating of armor and the vacuum chambers, set their teeth on edge. Then the rocket-ship was pointing directly down at one of the Lassans and Gloria snapped the key that released the artificial lightning.

A jagged beam of flame, intenser than the hottest furnace, leaped through the air, struck the green globe and sought the earth in a thousand tiny rivulets of light. For just a second the globe seemed unharmed. Then slowly, and almost majestically, it began to dissolve in mid-air, spouting flames at every pore. Fully ten miles down and beyond, the *Monitor* turned again, and not till then did the sound of the explosion reach them, a terrific rending thunderclap.

"See that?" cried Sherman. "That formation of theirs isn't so dumb. They've got it all ranged out. None of our ships can get at them without coming through at least one of those yellow rays and if we stay in them too long—blooie!"

They peered through the windows at the formation. Off to one side, they could make out the forms of two more rocket-ships, outlined against the sky. Behind and above them, pursued by the searching yellow beams, came the rest.

As they turned, they saw the gravity-beam shoot from one of the American ships, crumple uselessly against a green globe. Then they plunged in, again, firing the gravity beam earthward to work up the potential for another lightning discharge.

The hills below rocked and roared to the repeated shock. Trees fell in crashing ruin as lightning-bolt or infra-sound shivered them to bits. Great scars of burned earth and molten rock marked the spots where the gravity-beam struck the ground.

All round was a maze of yellow rays, lightning flashes and green globes that reeled, rose, fell, sometimes blowing up, sometimes giving ground, but always fighting back sternly and vigorously and always rising through the clear spring evening.

Murray Lee, at the rear of the ship, was the only one to see an American rocket-ship, caught and held for a few fatal moments by two yellow rays, slowly divest itself of its outer armor, then of its inner, go whirling to the earth, dissolved into its ultimate fragments by those irresistible pennons of sound.

Gloria Rutherford at the prow was the only one to see another caught bow-on in a yellow ray, reply by firing its gravity-beam right down the ray and into the green globe through the port from which the ray had issued. The ray went out—a spreading spot of flame appeared at the port and the great green globe crumpled into a little ball of flame before her eyes. But such events as these were the merest flashes in the close-locked combat.

For the most part they had time to do nothing but handle the controls, throw switches to and fro, shoot forth gravity-beam and lightning-flash in endless alternation at the Lassan ships of which there always appeared to be one more right before them as Sherman twisted and turned the *Monitor* with a skill that was almost uncanny.

Suddenly he pulled out. The four looked round. They were miles high. Below, half hidden in the dusk, were the red and brown roofs of a city.

"Had to get away for a minute," Sherman explained. "We were heating up from the speed. My word, but we're high up—at least forty-five thousand feet!"

"Yes, and getting higher," Ben pointed out. "Those green globes must be headed for the moon."

"I wouldn't be a bit surprised but what you're right," replied Sherman. "I'll bet that they think we can't navigate space and they're trying to get above us and then hang around and pop us when we have to land."

He shot the wings in again, worked the controls and they headed back toward the conflict.

It was less of a turmoil now, more of an ordered swing, charge, pass and charge again against the diminishing number of Lassan globes. Of the American rocket-ships Gloria could now count but two besides their own.

But the Lassans were not escaping unharmed. There were hardly a third as many as at the beginning and even as they approached another one disappeared in the vivid flash of the rocket's lightnings. Still the rest rose steadily.

They dived in. Gloria pressed the lightning key and another Lassan globe blew up. Then they were climbing again. Beneath them the night had come. The earth was a dark mass, far down, and from that enormous distance looked slightly dished out at the edges.

But though the earth was dark at that ultimate height of the atmosphere the sun had not yet set. Still the strange fight went on, higher and higher. The roar of the exhaust explosions died away behind them and Murray looked questioningly at Sherman.

"Out this far there isn't much air," he said. "Takes air to conduct sound. Wonder what they're up to anyway. All right, Gloria."

He dived at another Lassan and she pressed the lightning ray. But this time there was no flash.

"Who'd have thought it!" said Sherman, as he swung the *Monitor* round after the charge. "Of course—we're up so high that we've made a spark gap that even lightning won't jump. But sound rays won't be any good out here either."

Twenty-Three

The *Monitor* turned again, speeding back toward the remaining Lassan ships. With a shock of surprise Gloria noticed that there were only two. Down below them one of the last three American rocket-cruisers had spread her wings and was gliding gently toward the earth.

Like the *Monitor's*, her crew had evidently found the lightning flash worthless at the enormous altitude and was abandoning the battle till conditions became more favorable. The other rocket remained faithful, turned as they turned and charged up with them toward the last of the Lassans.

It was a weird scene. They had climbed so far that the earth was now perceptibly round beneath them; a vague line marked the westward progress of the sunset and beyond it the sun, an immense yellow ball, set with a crown of vividly red flames, hung in the inky-black heavens.

On the opposite side the stars made the sky a carpet of light across which the green globes moved like shadows, their undersides illumined by the sun.

As the *Monitor* approached the nearest globe seemed to be turning on its axis. Suddenly, out of the side that faced them, came the quick, stabbing beam of the light-ray, like the flicker of a sword. It struck the *Monitor* full on the prow.

There was a burning rain of sparks past the windows. The rocket-ship leaped and quivered and those within felt, rather than saw something give. Then, with a tremendous explosion, all the more horrible because utterly without sound, the great globe that had thrown the ray, burst into fragments.

At the same moment the *Monitor* began to fall. The sun went out. They were swallowed in a purple twilight as they plunged. The earth changed from a ball to a dish, from a dish to a plane, from a plane to a dark mass without form. In the mass vague lights and glimmerings of water came out and still their course was unchecked, still Sherman fought frantically with the useless controls.

Desperately Murray pressed the firing keys of the stern-rockets. Unchecked she drove on, almost straight down, plunging to certain destruction. The earth loomed nearer, nearer, the end seemed inevitable—.

Then Gloria saved them. In a moment of inspiration she threw on the searchlight and the automatic connector fired the gravity-beam. There was a shattering report. The course of the *Monitor* was halted and, bruised and broken, she tumbled over and over to the ground, safe but ruined.

"Suffering Lassans!" said Ben Ruby as they picked themselves out of the wreckage, "but that was a jar. What hit us anyway?"

Sherman pointed to Gloria, breathlessly. "Give the little girl a hand," he ejaculated. "She sure pulled us out of the fire that time."

"I'll say she did!" said Murray. "But what happened? I thought that light-ray of theirs wouldn't work on these ships."

"It won't—in air," said Sherman ruefully, surveying the wreck of the *Monitor*. "But the air blankets down the effect a lot. Out there we got the whole dose. Even then it shouldn't have hurt us so seriously but I expect a lot of our lead sheathing got jarred loose when we went through those yellow rays and when they let that light-ray go she leaked all over the place. Wonder what made that Lassan ship blow up like that though? I thought she sure had us."

"Oh!" said Ben. "I think maybe I did that. When the light-ray came on it occurred to me that the gravity-beam might go down their beam of light just as fast as it would down ours and they must have a porthole or something through their gravity-screen or they couldn't let the ray out. So I just let them have it."

"Look!" cried Gloria suddenly, pointing upward.

Far in the zenith above them they saw a point of light—a point that grew and spread and became definite as a great star. Then it became a shooting star, plunging earthward, and so great was its speed that even as they watched they could make out a green fragment, flame-warped in its midst.

"The last one!" said Sherman. "Wonder how they got her."

"Wonder what we do next," remarked Murray, practically.

They looked about them. They were on a hillside in a little clearing in a high, narrow valley. On every side were woods, dark and impenetrable. No landmarks, no roads were visible and the sky was darkening fast.

"The question," said Gloria, "is not where do we go but where are we going from."

"It might be most anywhere," remarked Murray.

"Well," Gloria offered, "I've been in a lot of mountains in my day, but I never saw any where following a stream didn't take you somewhere sooner or later. I vote we trail along with that brook there and see what happens."

"Bright thought," commented Ben. "Let's see what we can dig out of the wreck in the way of weapons."

"What for? If we meet any of the Lassans any weapon we got out of that mess wouldn't be much use. Wish we had a flashlight though."

Treading carefully but with a good deal of noise and confusion, they began to crash their way through the underbrush along the bank of the stream. At the foot of the valley it dived over a diminutive waterfall and then tumbled into another similar brook. Along the combined streams ran a road—a dirt road originally, now long untraveled, muddy and bad but still a road.

The night had become darker and darker, clouding over. But for the road they would have been completely lost. Finally, after skirting a hillcrest for a distance, the road dipped abruptly and as it did so, they passed out of the forest into a region cleared but not cultivated, with numerous close-cut stumps coming right to the roadside.

"But for the fact that it's a long way away," remarked Sherman, "I would say that this was the district around the Lassan headquarters."

"What makes you think it's a long way away?" asked Gloria. "Do you know where we are? Neither do I."

"By the nine gods of Clusium, I believe that's it at that!" said Sherman suddenly as the road turned past a place where a long scar of earth ran up the hillside, torn and blackened. "See—that looks exactly like the result of one of our gravity-beam shots! And there—isn't that the door?"

They were on the hillside now, directly ab___ had indicated. From above and in the da___ a cliff, breaking down rapidly to the valley. Sherman led them to one side, straight down the hill, and in another moment they were at its base. The great door through which the green balls had poured out that evening stood before them, a mighty arch reaching up into the dimness—and it was open.

"Looks like the boys haven't come home to supper yet," said Gloria in an awed whisper.

"Yes, and a lot of them aren't coming, either," replied Murray in a similar tone.

"Listen, you three," said Sherman. "You run along and build some more monitors and go get whatever comes out of here. Me, I'm going to have a whirl at this door. The swellest girl in the world is in there or was—and I'm going to find her."

"Nothing doing, old man," said Ben. "If you go in we go in too—except Gloria."

"What's the matter with me?" she demanded. "I'm made of the same kind of machinery you are, aren't I? And I'm good enough to run your foolish fighting machine. Don't be a dope." And she stepped forward.

The blue-domed hall that gave directly on the outer air had disappeared since Sherman and Marta Lami had raced out of it. In its place was an enormous tunnel, lined apparently with some metal, for its sides were smooth and shimmering.

The portion they entered was lightless but it curved as it ran down and around the curve they could see the faint reflection of a light somewhere further along the passage. Their feet echoed oddly in the enormous silence of the place. There seemed nothing within.

"Boy!" whispered Murray to Gloria. "If one of those green globes comes back now it will squash us flatter than a stage bankroll. This is the craziest thing we ever did."

"Right," she said, "but what the heck? I came along for the ride. Look, what's that?"

Before them, around the bend of the passage, they could see another door from which the light which glittered along the tunnel was streaming. In the opening stood a man, or what seemed to be a man, facing, fortunately, inwards.

After a moment's cautious peering, Sherman pronounced him one of the apeman slaves. He wore a thought-helmet and had some kind of a weapon in his hand. The four held a whispered conference.

"Listen," said Sherman, "we've got to jump that baby before he does anything. I think he's got one of those small light-guns. Now, who's got a knife?"

A search of pockets revealed that Murray Lee had the only one in the company.

"Never mind," said Sherman. "One is enough. Now we three . . . . . . him. The main thing is not to let him see us. If . . . . . . him quick. Remember, there's a Lassan at the other end of the line and the Lassan is getting everything he thinks.

"He doesn't think very fast but don't take chances. If he sees us you hop in, Murray, and cut the wire that leads out of his helmet and short-circuit it. They may have it fixed so that it won't short-circuit by now but I don't think so.

"If he doesn't see us before we jump him clap your hands over his eyes, Ben, and I'll try to get the helmet off him and pass out some information to the Lassan at the other end that will keep him quiet. But the main thing is to get that gun first. Everybody understand?"

Three heads nodded in unison.

"All right. Come on."

They crept up the passage together avoiding touching hands lest the ring of metal should warn the sentry. As they approached they could see the room he looked out on was one of the familiar blue-domed halls. The passage ended sharply some six feet above its floor.

"Taking no chances on more escapes," thought Sherman.

The hall was of enormous size. There were machines in one corner of the floor. In another stood one of the green globes, half finished, with spidery trellises of red metal outlining what would be the surface of the sphere. Around it helmeted mechanical men came and went busily. The rest of the hall, for all its vast extent, was completely empty. At the far end was a row of doors—high on the far side an opening that looked like a door but had no obvious purpose.

This much they saw. Then the sentry stirred. Before he had time to turn Ben Ruby launched himself in a football tackle for his legs, bringing the ape-man down with a crash.

As he fell Sherman snatched at the helmet and Gloria at the light-gun, which had dropped from his fingers, while Murray pinioned the struggling creature's arms. In a moment Sherman found the finger holes in the helmet, pressed, and it came loose in his hands. The ape-man ceased to struggle.

"Let him up now, folks," said Sherman, "give him a swift kick and point him toward the door. He won't come back." He rapidly adjusted the thought-helmet to his own head.

The Lassan at the other end was evidently disturbed. He had received the sound of the crash from the ape-man's brain and was asking querulously what it meant.

"What has happened?" the thought demanded insistently. "What is it that struck you? Have the fighting machines re turned? Show a picture of what you see. Are the slaves esc ing?"

"Everything's all right," Sherman sent back. "S broke loose down below and I stumbled trying to He closed his eyes, forming a mental picture everything in order, then one of the passa and detached the helmet, motioning to Murray for the knife. An instant's sawing and the device short-circuited with a fizzing of blue sparks.

"That will give that one a headache for a while," he remarked. "We'll have to hurry though. When he comes to, he'll investigate and then there'll be trouble."

"What's that?" asked Gloria, pointing across the hall at the aperture high up in the wall. A gleaming beak had been thrust out and the bright, intelligent eye of one of the dodo birds was regarding them malevolently from the opening.

"Shoot—quick!" said Sherman. "For heaven's sake! They're telepathic. They'll have every Lassan in the place after us."

Gloria fumbled a second with the gun, located the finger hole, sent a spurt of light flying across the room. It missed the head but found its mark somewhere in the body of the bird, for there was a squawk and the head disappeared. Sherman vaulted down the six-foot drop, landing with a bang.

"Come on!" he cried. "Short-circuit every wire you can find. Tear them loose if you can't cut them any other way. Then make for the middle door at the back."

They ran across the hall toward the work benches. It seemed enormous, like a race in a dream, in which one seems to make no progress whatever. But the workers, driven by the thoughts of the controlling Lassans, were incapable of attending to anything else unless it was forced on their attention.

As they approached the benches, however, one flat-faced ape-man almost ran into them. His face took on an expression of puzzled inquiry and at the same moment a figure whose carriage plainly showed it to be human stepped down toward them from the half-completed green globe. Gloria paused, leveled her light-gun at the ape-man and his face vanished in a spray of fire. The human advanced slowly as though struggling against some force that was too strong for him. Sherman reached him first, wrenched the helmet from his head and dropping it on the floor stamped on it till the fine mechanism was irretrievably ruined. The mechanical human fell to his knees.

"Who are you?" he asked.

Sherman said, "Which way to the living cages? Do you know Marta Lami?"

The man shook his head like one recovering from a dream. "don't know," he said. "They had the helmet on me for periods. I don't know nothing. We came through that the little automobiles." He indicated a door behind machines.

urgent but Sherman paused to instruct them be another sentry at the door. Pop him first, your knife. Ben, get anything you can and se birds around here. There are some more wires leading out of the machines. Be sure to get them, too. You might let loose something important. We'll try to get you another gun."

Twenty-Four

Impassively, oblivious of the invasion about them, the workers kept on at their machines like ants when their nest is broken open. Sherman and Gloria dodged around one of them, avoiding the direct line of sight of the robot who worked at it and walked rapidly toward the door giving on the cartracks. The man on duty had no weapon but paid them no attention, being occupied in watching a car just sliding in to the station.

"It's a shame," began Gloria.

"Shoot!" insisted Sherman and the light-ray struck him in the back of the neck, fusing head and neck to a single mass. As he sank to the floor he turned partly over.

"Good heavens, it's Stevens!" said Gloria, "the man who organized the rebellion against Ben Ruby in New York and brought the dodos down on us."

"Never mind—hurry," her companion urged in a fever of activity. The doors of the car were opening and half a dozen mechanical men stepped out, most with the foolish visages and shambling steps of the ape-men—but two had the upright walk which showed them human.

"Listen, everybody," called Sherman. "We're from outside. We're trying to bust up this place. Get back in the car, quick, and help us."

Suiting the action to the word he leaped for the first compartment, reached it just as it was closing and wedged himself inside.

The car had a considerable run to make. In the dimly-lit compartment Sherman was conscious of turns—right, left, right again—and of a steady descent. He wondered vaguely whether he had taken the right method—whether the cage rooms lay near one another or were widely separated.

At all events the diversion in the hall of the green globes would hold the attention of the Lassans. The short-circuiting of so many lines would hamper their methods of dealing with the emergency.

The car came to a stop. Sherman heard a door or two open but his own did not budge and he had no needle to stir it. He must wait, hoping that Gloria had not been isolated from him. She had the ray-gun at all events and would not be helpless. Then the door opened again.

He was released into a cage that seemed already occupied, and one look told him that his companion was an ape-man.

"Gloria!" he called.

"Right here," came the cheerful answer from two cages down. "This is a swell thing you got me into. How do we get out of here?"

"Have you got a pin or needle of any kind?" he asked.

"Why—yes. Turn your back." She did something mysterious among her feminine garments and held up an open safety-pin for him to see across the intervening cage.

"Stick your arm through the bars and see if you can toss it down the track. If I don't get it you'll have to blast your way out with the light-gun but I don't like to do that. Don't know how many shots it holds and we need them all."

She swung with that underarm motion which is the nearest any woman can achieve to a throw. The pin struck the gleaming car-rail, skidded, turned, came to rest before Sherman's cage. He reached for it but the ape-man in the cage, who had been watching with interested eyes, was quicker. Fending Sherman off with one huge paw he reached one of his feet through the bars for the object and held it up before his eyes admiringly.

Sherman grabbed but this only fixed the ape-man in his evident opinion that the object he held was of value. He gripped it all the tighter, turned an amiable face toward Sherman and gibbered. Losing patience, Sherman lifted an iron foot and kicked him, vigorously and with purpose, in the place where kicks do the most good.

The ape-man pitched forward, dropping the fascinating pin, then rose and came toward Sherman, his expression clearly indicating his intention of tearing the American limb from limb. The cage was narrow, the ape-man the bigger of the two. Sherman thought hard and fast. The oilball!

He leaped for the lectern, snatched it open, seized the ape-man's oilball and held it aloft as though to throw it out into the corridor. With a wail of anguish the simian clutched at the precious object. Sherman squeezed it enough to let a little stream run forth, holding it just out of his reach and, as he stabbed for it again, tossed it back into a corner of the cell. The ape-man leaped upon it covetously and Sherman bent over the bars, fumbling in his nervous haste to unlock them.

Luckily the safety-pin fitted. With a subdued click the bars swung inward and he was out in the corridor. Another moment and Gloria was free also.

"Any more people in here?" Sherman called. Three voices answered and he hurried from cage to cage, setting them free as the warning blue lights that prohibited shouting began to flicker around the roof.

"Come on," he called. "We must get out of here quick!"

They hesitated a moment between the two doors, chose that at the upper end. As they raced through it they heard a panel clash somewhere. The Lassans were investigating.

They were in one of the passages through which the cars ran, with alternate bars of light and dark across it marking the termination of side-passages.

"*Look!*" said Gloria. Into the cage-room they had just quitted a car was coming, its featureless front gliding noiselessly along the track.

"In here," said Sherman, pulling the others after him down the nearest lighted passage. Followed by the other four Sherman moved steadily along to the right, where the passage ended at a door.

"What now?" said someone.

"In," decided Gloria. "Likely to be a cage-room as not."

Sherman searched for the inevitable finger holes, found them and pressed. The door swung back on—

A Lassan reclining at ease on one of the curious twisted benches beside which stood a tall jar of the same yellow-flecked green material they had seen the others devouring. The room was blue-domed but very small and its walls were covered with soft green hangings in pendulous drops.

A thought-helmet was on the elephant-man's head. Its other end was worn by one of the mechanical people, whose back was to the door as they entered and who appeared to be working some kind of machine that punched little holes of varying shape in a strip of bright metal.

As the five Americans pressed into the room the Lassan rose and reached for his ray-gun. Gloria pushed the one she held into his face and he relaxed with a little squeal of terror while Sherman reached into his pouch and secured the weapon. As he did so the Lassan reached up and snapped loose the thought-helmet; the metal figure turned and gazed at them.

"*Marta!*"

"The boy friend!"

The Lassan was very old. His skin was almost white and seamed with sets of diminutive wrinkles. As he regarded the two mechanical people locked in each other's embrace an expression of puzzlement and distaste came over his features, giving place to one of cool and lofty dignity as he perceived that Gloria did not mean to kill him on the spot. Lifting his trunk he motioned imperiously toward the thought-helmet, which Marta had cast aside, then set the other end of it on his own head.

Sherman's face became grave and, following the Lassan's direction, he picked up the helmet and fitted it on his head. The thought that came through it gave a feeling of dignity and power such as he had never experienced before.

"By what right," it demanded, "do you invade the room of scientific composition? Why are you not in your cages? You know you will receive the punishment of the yellow lights in the greater degree for this unauthorized invasion. Save yourself further punishment now by retiring quietly. You can take my life, it is true, but I am old and my life is of no value. Think not that I am the only Lassan in the universe."

"Sorry," Sherman gave him back, "but this is a rebellion. You are not familiar with the history of this planet or you would know that Americans can't be anybody's slaves. Let us go in peace and we will let you return to your own planet."

"Let us go!" came the Lassan's answer. "Your obstinate presumption surprises me. Do you think that the Lassans of Rigel, the highest race in the universe, will let go what they have once grasped?"

"You will or we'll jolly well make you," replied the American. "Do you think your silly green globes are going to do you any good? The last one fell beside us tonight."

Sherman could sense the sudden wave of panic in the Lassan's thought at this unexpected answer. He had evidently assumed that they were from the underground labor battalions and were not familiar with events outside. But he rallied nobly.

"And do you imagine, foolish creature of a lower race, that the green globes are our last resource? Even now I have perfected a device that will wipe your miserable people from the planet. But if it did not, rather would we Lassans perish in the flames of a ruined world than abandon a task once undertaken. We who can mold the plastic flesh to enduring metal and produce machines that have brains. We who can control the great substance that underlies all life and matter."

"Well, here's one task you're going to abandon," Sherman thought back. "We, who can call lightning from the skies, are going to give you a terrible sock on the—trunk if you don't. If you doubt it try and find how many Lassans live after today's battle. Go on back where you came from. You're not wanted in this world."

"You know or should know the law of evolution," replied the Lassan. "The weaker and less intelligent must ever give way before the stronger. By the divine right of—" His flow of thought stopped suddenly, changed to a wild tumult of panic. Sherman looked up. Round the rim of the blue dome, where it stood above the hangings, a string of lights was winking oddly, in a strange uneven rhythm.

"God of the Lassans, deliver us!" the thought that reached his own was saying. "The tanks are broken! The light is loose!" Then suddenly his mind was closed and when it opened again it had taken on a new calmness and dignity and a certain godlike strength.

"I do not know how or where,'" it told Sherman, "but an accident has happened. Perhaps an accident produced by your strange and active race. The connections have broken. The tanks of the substance of life in the bowels of this mountain have broken and the whole is set free. It is hard to see the labor of centuries thus destroyed—to see you, creatures of a lower race, inherit a world so divinely adapted to the rule of intelligence.

"For in this accident the whole of our race must perish if you have told the truth about the destruction of our green globes. We called in all the Lassans from your world for the work of the destruction of your armies.

"Yes, you told the truth. Your mind is open—I can see it. We are lost—there is no hope remaining. It means destruction or the metal metamorphosis for every living Lassan and there will be none to endow them with the life in metal we have given you.

"Perhaps it was our own fault. Your curious race, for all its defects, has certain qualities of intelligence, above all that strange quality of activity and what you call courage. If we could have summoned up the same activity—if we had possessed the same courage to attack against odds—this would not have happened.

"It is our failure that we have depended too much on naked intellect, learned to do too many things through the hands of our servants. Had Lassans been at the controls of our fighting ships, instead of the automatons we used, you would never have conquered them so easily.

"Be that as it may. We have lost and you have won. I can show myself more generous than you would have been and thus can gain a victory over you. If you would escape follow the car-track straight on to where it forks, then take the left-hand turning.

"If you would be restored to your former and imperfect and repulsive form—though I cannot conceive why you should, being permanently fixed in beautiful and immortal metal—do not run away but await the coming of the substance of life in the outer hall or passage. Be careful not to approach it too closely or to touch it, so that you may receive the emanation only.

"It is this emanation, surrounding our space ship that produced your present form, which we changed to machinery by our surgery. It so acts on the metal of which you are composed that it will reverse the case. As for me I am old and tired. Already the walls of this place tremble to the coming of my doom. Leave me before I regret what I have told you."

He reached with his trunk and disconnected the thought-helmet. Standing up, with a certain high dignity, he pointed to the door.

Relieved of the helmet Sherman could hear a confused roaring like that on the day when Marta Lami and he had short-circuited the mining machine.

"Come on," he called to the rest, dropping the helmet. "Hell's let loose. We've got to hurry."

Outside the roaring was perceptibly louder and seemed to be approaching. As they leaped down to the track a faint glow was borne to them redly along the rail. The ape-men in the cage room they had escaped from were howling and beating the bars of theirs cages, with no blue lights to forbid them.

The track was slippery—Marta Lami and the three they had released from the cage room, unshod. Sherman gripped her by the hand. "Hurry, *hurry!*" he panted, pulling her along.

They passed another passage, down which a door stood open. The soft light that normally illuminated the place was flickering wildly. They caught a glimpse of three or four Lassans within, stirring about, rushing from place to place, trying this connection and that. The dull sound behind them increased. The track grew steeper.

"What about the rest?" gasped Gloria, running by his side.

"Don't know," he answered. "They did something. The whole place is coming down."

As they rounded a corner the track forked before them. Remembering the Lassan's parting instructions, Sherman led them to the left, passed another passage mouth and they found themselves in a small blue-domed hall, empty save for a single car that stood on the track.

There was just room to squeeze past it where the passage began again at the other end. And as they made it the roaring sound changed to a series of explosions, sharp and clear. The ground trembled, seemed to tilt. The car slid backward into the passage they had just vacated.

Ten feet, twenty-five feet more—and they were on the platform leading to the hall of the green globes. Sherman swung himself up, offered a hand to Marta. In a moment the others were beside them and they were darting for the door. The ground was trembling again, shock after shock. Something fell with a crash as they raced across the platform and into the hall.

Within all was confused darkness and a babble of sound. A dodo screamed somewhere. An ape-man ran past them, gibbering, mad with fright, and dived to the track. Sherman ran across the hall, followed by Marta and the three he had released. Gloria halted.

"Murray!" she cried, *"Murray!"* and then lifted the light-gun and sent a pencil of fire screeching to the roof. There was an answering shock as something tumbled from the ceiling.

"Murray!" she called again, at the top of her voice. Behind them, through the platform, something fell with a crash and a long red flame licked through the door, throwing tall shadows and weird lights across the bedlam within.

"Here!" came a voice and Gloria turned to see Murray and Ben running toward her.

"Come on," she said, "hurry. The works is busted."

They made the doorway just as Sherman was pulling Marta up the six-foot step. Ben and Murray lifted Gloria in their arms, tossed her up. The red flame in the background had given place to a white one and a boiling white mass of something was sending a long tongue creeping across the floor.

Willing arms snatched at those of Ben and Murray, pulling them upward to safety. They turned to run down the tunnel.

"No!" cried Sherman. *"Stick!* It's all right. The old bloke told me so."

There was another explosion and a great white cloud rolled toward them above the liquid tide. Then they lapsed into unconsciousness.

Murray Lee yawned and sat up.

The others lay around him in curious piled attitudes as though they had dropped off to sleep in the midst of something. He noted with a shock of surprise that Ben Ruby's face, turned in his direction, was not metal, but good honest flesh and blood. He gazed at his own hands—flesh and blood likewise. He looked around.

The hall of the blue dome had vanished. A tangled mass of rock, cemented in some gray material, was before them, obscure in the darkness. At the other end was the passage, its ceiling fallen here and there, its sides caved in. But a stream of light showed that an opening still led to the outside.

He bent over and shook Gloria. She came to with a start, looked about her, said with an air of surprise, "Oh, have I been asleep? Why, what's happened to you Murray? You need a shave." Then she felt of her own face and found it smooth again.

"For Heaven's sake!" she ejaculated.

The sound brought the rest bolt upright. Sherman looked round at the others, then at the passage, smiled with satisfaction.

"That old Lassan," he remarked, "told me the metal evolution would reverse if we got the emanation without letting the stuff touch us. Well, he was a sport."

"Yes but—" said Marta Lami, standing up and feeling of herself. "Look what they did to us. My toes are flexible and my figure bulges in such queer places. I'll never be able to dance again. Oh, well, I suppose it doesn't matter—I'll be marrying my chum here anyway." She took Sherman's hand and he blushed with embarrassment.

"Good idea," said Murray Lee and looked hard at Gloria.

She nodded and turned her head.

"Ho, hum," said Ben Ruby. "The dictator of New York seems to be *de trop*. How does one get out of here?"